LANDLOCKED IN FOREIGN SKIN

A SAPPHIC SCI-FI NOVELLA

DREW HUFF

Edited by Candace Nola

Cover art and design by Evangeline Gallagher

ISBN: 979-8-9907906-6-7 (ebook)

ISBN: 979-8-9907906-7-4 (paperback)

To those imprisoned in obsolete skins, lives, values, and ideals,
To the smothered,
To the lost:

I see you.

PRAISE FOR DREW HUFF

"*Landlocked In Foreign Skin* is a blend of far future science and ancient folkloric religion told through a sapphic unravelling identity mystery filled with manipulation and adaptation—sharp and quirky."

— AI JIANG, BRAM STOKER AND NEBULA AWARD-WINNING AUTHOR OF *LINGHUN* AND *I AM AI*

"*Landlocked In Foreign Skin* is a surprising blend of myth, sci-fi, and horror that will keep you up all night. Drew Huff is a fearless storyteller, and The Fisherman is the kind of character who you'll never forget."

— BONNIE JO STUFFLEBEAM, AUTHOR OF *GRIM ROOT*

"*Free Burn* is a high-octane horror novel that's as full of heart as it is disturbing. It gripped me from the first page and broke me over and over again. This book is everything."

— STEPH NELSON, AUTHOR OF *THE FINAL SCENE* AND *THE VEIN*

"If you imagine a William S. Burroughs fever dream while *Edward Scissorhands* plays in the background, you'll have a vague idea of what lives in the pages of *Free Burn*. Drew Huff's explosive debut spins the legend of Bonnie and Clyde into a story that explores the depth of trauma with unapologetic weirdness. A manic, propulsive tale of sweat, blood, and…other bodily fluids."

— BRENNAN LAFARO, AUTHOR OF *NOOSE* AND
THE SLATTERY FALLS TRILOGY

"Jaw-dropping in its uniqueness, stunning in its prose, and captivating in tone, concept, and approach; *Free Burn* is a perfect example of why I am a reader. Drew Huff is one author that other authors NEED to be reading. Stories like this are why I love to read; authors like Drew Huff endlessly inspire me to write. Read *Free Burn*. Read Drew Huff. She will be a force in the fiction world, soon."

— CANDACE NOLA, AUTHOR OF *DESPERATE WISHES*

"Drew Huff roars out of the gate with this strong debut, a radical reinvention of the road novel with shades of Katherine Dunn's *Geek Love* and Joe Hill's *Horns*

— DUNCAN RALSTON, AUTHOR OF *WOOM* AND
GHOSTLAND

CONTENTS

CONTENT WARNINGS

Self-injury, suicide attempt, suicidal ideation, homophobia, violence, body horror, LGBT conversion therapy, brain damage, profane language, and explicit sexual content.

CHAPTER 1

Transcript from the E.N.S Princess Recording Log.

IT STARTS WITH THE PAIN—SOMETHING jabbing through your back, radiating heat, tearing—

(*light*)

And ends with it.

"Take it off," one of Them says, voice higher pitched than the others.

You can't generate vocal cords fast enough. You grow them later. Too late. Metal gleams in Jove-light. Jove's overhead, through glass. You're pulse-pulsing, feeling sick, straining for something not-there.

Pain burns in a line. Digs.

Something probes.

"Tear it off, dear. Like a sweater."

You sprout the right eyes just before they tear your skin off and see: orange-clad bodies (*human*) encircling you, tiny by comparison. Ten sets of limbs nudge you.

Tear?

You parse the words, remember vague language passed to you by a Friend.

"Get it out," repeats the clear, high-pitched voice.

They start peeling. They do. All of Them rip off your shell of fat, of skin, reduce you down to a mewling, choking unformed mass of flesh.

One of Them kneels by you. Touches you. "You know how to look. Do it."

A female. All mammary glands, curves, waving hair. Eyes like deep ice. Lungs. Cephalized head, singular. A brain.

You form. She blinks, and something in your new, centralized head goes, *Good.* She's happy. Something warm strokes your face.

She bares her teeth in a *(good)* way, *(smiling)*. They've already bustled your skin away by the time you think to ask.

"Where. Where is my skin?"

"It's safe with me," she says, "I'm Dame Isobel."

She pronounces it like Dah-may, and her expression twitches briefly as she says it. Dame Isobel. The expression isn't natural. It's artificial. Made. Composed. You don't like it.

You force out words, garbled at first. "Want. What do you want?"

Her smile warps, now not right *(unpleasant) (bad)*.

"I want *you.*"

CAN YOU FATHOM THAT, listener?

I doubt it.

So.

Dame Isobel tore off...not my skin. Not some inert flesh-wrapper, devoid of insulation. Call it an outer layer. Porous, with a long memory for organic matter. Malleable. Imagine:

You swirl under ice, feel the pressure ebb and flow while Jove seethes magnetic storms, and your outer layer—call it a hide—transmutes in response, a million genetic memories stored within. It's a fragment of Aeter, the Dreaming Impulse, who's only sometimes conscious. Aeter, the eternal parent. Aeter, who thought, gestated, and shifted reality as They saw fit. As They see fit.

And Dame Isobel called Aeter the "Wishing Fish."

So.

I gasped on the deck, skin prickling from the (*cold!*)

"I want you," Dame Isobel said. "Change again. Into something pretty."

"I—I can't."

She blinked. "You're a Fisherman. That's what you do."

My voice didn't sound right. It kept getting higher. I couldn't swallow the lump in my throat. "It's in my—skin? I can't do it. It's in—"

I can't get out of HERE! Can't breathe.

A nasty throbbing in my new ears. Heat.

(*Stuck*)

"I'm stuck. Give it back," I said.

Dame Isobel twined her fingers through mine. She smiled a (*good*) smile.

"But then you'd leave me. You wouldn't want that," she said. "Come on. See the ship."

Did she want seabed metals like the other humans?

"Return it. After," I said.

"Of course, dear," she said.

She did not.

"We've never had a Fisherman as a guest before," Dame Isobel said.

It would've brought me pleasure to snap at her, even with those fruitless teeth I had, but rope bound me. A sticky rectangle thing covered my current mouth. I tried again to grow another mouth. Couldn't.

(this is not MY skin, this is NOT my body)

Water filled my eyes.

They'd escorted me to a closed, solid area, put something over my single mouth, and tied the things at the end of my (arms), my (wrists) to something. I couldn't move. Couldn't shift out. Despite my attempts to change and slip away—knowing the impossibility of it, without my hide-skin-sheath—I'd achieved nothing. I sat. Useless twin eyes saw little in the darkness. Stupid eyes. Blind to heat or radiation. In the colder (winter?) portion of the year, I would grow better eyes: radiation perceived as glowing color, heat bands visible. Darkness didn't exist. Darkness implied a nothing, an invisible. To not exist. Everything existed. We changed to perceive it.

What kind of stupid, inert form was I currently trapped in?

Isobel's voice grew teeth. "Can you understand me?"

Chilled air brushed my skin from the ceiling rectangle. The (vent). The ceiling rectangle where the air came from was called a vent.

"Can you speak?" Isobel asked.

I sat in a metal box, and she stood over me. Jove seethed overhead, unseen. Tendon-colored cord bound my wrists together, snaking through an arc of metal fused to the floor.

Dame Isobel touched a finger to the sticky thing obliterating my mouth. It slipped off and fell to the ground. The sticky looked slimy now. Mucous? Organic or—

(chemical?)

I prodded the thing. It remained inert. Lifeless. Tasteless.

The word came to me: Tape.

"Fisherman?"

I blurted, "Where is my skin-hide-sheath—?"

Took a breath, decided that *skin* was the most accurate word.

"Where is my skin, Dame Isobel? You promised to return it so I could leave," I said.

"You haven't had the tour yet."

"I don't want it."

She put her hands on her hips and stuck her lower lip out. Blue fabric covered her form, fluttering in the air from the vent. Was that blue material her skin? I ran my *(palm)* over it. *(Silk) (organic)* tasted a smell of chemical, *(plant) (insect)*. A ghost-image flickered through my mind: An oblong *(green)* flat thing being chewed by another oblong thing, *(bug)*, a fat living *(larva)* like my mid-year *(summer)* form?

How bizarre. The green flat thing was a form of plant life that grew above Home *(water)* and practiced efficient photosynthesis, instead of the typical radiosynthesis. The fat living thing was a lifeform that changed shape depending on its age. *Silk-worm*. Yes. That was the word. The larval form held similarities to my mid-year form. Interesting. Interesting! What a fun concept. It tasted good. The humans used the silkworms to make garments. Dame Isobel wore a gown composed of an alien lifeform's discarded shell *(cocoon)*, unwound and woven, dyed with chemicals that made the material reflect light of a certain wavelength *(color)* and the range of this dress's material fell within what humans classified as "blue".

I admit it: I smiled. All the others would covet these facts once I returned home. Nobody else knew these things except me, and I'd obtain *so many* secrets, concepts, ideas, and genetic memories in return for my knowledge. Oh yes. My tongue flickered out from between my lips and wet them.

"Why would you want to leave?" Isobel finally said.

First I have to get Home. Then I'll trade my knowledge. Focus.

Isobel's face crumpled. It had turned red in the interim. Interesting.

"I don't live here. If you try to turn my skin into one of your dresses like you did with the silkworms, I will skin you. I will return your kindness," I said.

"You're being silly."

"Give me my skin and let me go home."

She smiled. "But you just got here!"

"I'm in pain. I don't normally maintain one form for this long. Let me go. Please."

"Do you want to see it? Your skin?"

I got to my feet. "Yes."

She used a metal thing (*knife*) to cut the rope. My wrists remained bound. I held them out for her to free, but she put the knife back in its sheath. Knives. Humans used those. Someone I knew had told me what it felt like to be stabbed by one—mining ship, callous workers, a net—but we ignored humans, mostly. Humans called us Fishermen. We ignored them. They built cities atop the ice, cities on a waterless plain we had no use for and rarely went to. Most humans, I believed, didn't think we were intelligent, let alone (*sapient*). Yes, that's the word. Sapient. We never took on sapient form—why would we? I heard someone in a pod near the far poles did, once, to communicate, but they weren't someone I knew well. I'd heard stories. Generations of invaders had grown, bred, and died from first contact to now. When the men with testing equipment and water tanks and shred-proof nets hunted for us, we killed them, but not otherwise.

Too stringy. They didn't taste good.

"You're my special guest," Isobel said.

"This doesn't happen. I don't belong here."

"Silly Fisherman."

A door opened. Orange light spilled in from the hallway outside. Silhouetted in the light, a male figure lurked. Plant-smell (*pine*) tinged the air.

Isobel put her hand on the small of my back and nudged. I

did nothing. She walked to the door, turned, and stood there, staring at me.

"Well?" Isobel said.

"Hm?"

"Follow me. You're supposed to follow me," she said.

"Oh."

I followed. So did the male. He wore a blue thing that covered him from collarbone to ankles (*jumpsuit*). His skin was darker than Isobel's, his facial features different. Silver hair curled from his head and chin. Yellow beads studded his braided chin hair. Guns and a knife glinted on his belt.

I pointed to him. "Is he here for a reason?"

"Don't mind Gavin. He's here to make sure we're safe."

"I'd be safer if I had my skin."

"We're going to see it right now."

She grazed her fingers along my arm. Something twanged between my legs, inside me; it went *(good) (yes)*, it was the taste of sweet, the whisper-sweet coil of a warm current, *(good good good)*.

My skin prickled. Bumps quivered from the flesh.

She saw that. Her smile stretched further, making her eyes crinkle. Saliva glistered her white, white teeth.

"What's your name?" Isobel asked.

"Name?"

"What do people call you?"

"Fishermen."

"What does your family call you?"

"Aeter calls us all Little One."

"The Wishing Fish?"

"Huh?"

I'd made a sound. It came out of me. Shock possessed a sound in this form. Interesting.

"The Wishing Fish! Is it named Aeter? Is it—"

"Why am I still here?"

Isobel guided us up a stairwell to another door. Letters glowed above the door. Gavin opened it for Isobel. We ventured down an orange-painted hallway lined with windowless doors. Nodules of metal patterned the floor. Vents droned. Clattering sounds came from behind the doors: footsteps, talking, shuffling paper, slamming drawers. A smell of human polluted the sterile air. Faintly, through walls—ice crunched, water slapped. This ship. It was cutting through Home's ice as it journeyed.

A sharp poke. "…what do you like to eat?"

"Matter. Meat. Flesh. Plant," I said. "It depends."

"You're my special dinner guest."

I didn't know what *special* meant, but it couldn't be good. Isobel's pupils dilated whenever she said *special*.

"Where is my skin?" I said.

She stuck her lip out again. "People don't talk to me like that."

"I'm not a person."

"How does your skin work? Tell me. Tell me stories."

We arrived at a gray door with blinking red lights. Gavin gestured at the lights. They turned green, something went click, and the door creaked open, exposing a white expanse. Latticework cluttered the high ceiling. Besides a gray couch, the area held nothing. We entered. Our footsteps echoed.

"This is the ENS *Princess's* recreation room," Isobel said. "The walls have images of Europa projected onto them when it's being used…oh, you'd love it, and there's tables set up—"

"Europa?"

"You know. Here. This moon."

"Home. This is Home."

"Of course it is."

Walking. What an inefficient form of locomotion. Too little gravity here. No reassuring tug to anchor me, keep me tethered to Home. Home. Home—

More water filled my eyes. I tasted it. Saltwater. Proteins. Tangy hormones (*cortisol*).

If I pretended to be interested, she might return my skin.

I asked, "ENS. *Princess?*"

Isobel gripped my arm, digging her long claws into the meat. Gems sparkled on the blue claws. Nails. Whatever they were, they tasted (*wrong*).

"That's this ship. My family's called the Dame family. Dahmay. We mine gold from the seabed. Renault's been trying to farm genetically engineered fish, but they keep vanishing," she said.

"Oh, those tiny things? We ate them. Before they could reproduce. Aeter told us to," I said.

She yanked my arm, forcing me to stop. "Told you to?"

"Aeter wanted us to be fed. They wanted the unnatural life gone."

"So it talks to you. Does it grant wishes?"

"What's a wish?"

Her eyes glazed. "Because I need one. I need a wish so much. She needs to live. You know? Have you ever loved someone so much you'd die for them? Well. She did that for me. Kind of. She needs my help. I need to fix her. She's my friend. My special friend—"

"Dame Isobel, the elevator," Gavin said.

Aeter, help me. Help me.

CHAPTER 2

The ENS *Princess* boasted five floors, two kitchens—
one of which was for Dame Isobel and her personal
chef, Cherise—a brig built to contain a human, six months'
worth of food and water, incendiary weaponry, the cargo hold,
Dame Isobel's mansion-quarters, Dame Isobel's maid, Celia,
such a good friend, Fisherman!—an airlock through which a
human in a robotic submersible could access the ocean in case
external ship repairs were needed, a viewing deck with a
massive window and comfortable furniture, the recreation
room, and additional living quarters designed for one-hundred-
and-fifty crewmen. No *(wastewater)* containment. They dumped
their wastewater, saliva and soaps and chemicals and foreign
bacteria and all, into Home.

"How many crewmen are currently here?" I asked, as we
passed another door-lined, orange hallway.

Cabin C, this one. Thirty bunks, fifteen rooms. Fifteen
doors.

"Oh, wow…uh, Gavin? How many men onboard?" Isobel
asked.

"Thirty-two, ma'am. Including me."

She smiled. "Fisherman, what it's like to live underwater? Do you have friends? Family?"

"Friends."

"Loved ones?"

"Yes. We all know each other. They will be confused. I should go back. I need my skin," I said.

She laughed. We went down five flights of stairs.

This ship was too empty. Thirty-two crewmen in a ship for a hundred and fifty. Humans didn't make decisions like that when it came to resources.

Dame Isobel continued on and on about the ENS *Princess*. Pressure pushed down on me; we'd gone a hundred feet below the ice surface. Machinery groaned, unmuffled by walls. It dulled the sound of her voice.

What I did not hear or see: Mining rigs, drills, or equipment.

What was this ship *actually* doing?

I contorted my mouth into a grin like Isobel's, attempting to mimic her. "Do you normally live on this ship?"

"No, silly! I live in the Callisto Manor, in Brilliante—I can't wait to show you the Manor someday—"

"I'm leaving after this tour."

"Well. Someday. When you come back to visit."

"That won't happen," I said.

Her face twisted as if I'd struck her. Then she made the manic smile reappear.

"I have an artificial lake full of sea bass, and another one for salmon," she said. "The only source of fresh fish in three states. You'll love my salmon. I have a friend. You need to meet her. She'll heal. How do you heal? Tell me about the Wishing Fish."

"Aeter isn't a resource, Dame Isobel."

"It grants wishes. That's what all the legends say."

She gripped my hand. She squeezed. It hurt.

"Tell me about the Wishing Fish. Where is it?" Isobel said.

"Where is my skin? Give me my skin, and I'll tell you. Maybe

I'll even show you. I'll drag you there. Under the water," I said. "And then I'll *eat you.*"

"Oh, great!"

Was Isobel brain-damaged? I scrutinized her eyes. They seemed bright and active, but what did I know about humans? I'd never seen one this close. They couldn't breathe outside. Couldn't breathe underwater. They froze within seconds of existing, unless suited in *(skin?)* Protective gear, that was the word, suits.

Because I'd roughly mimicked Dame Isobel when I'd taken this form, fragments of her copied brain kept surfacing. Half-memories. The taste of salt, smell of *(rubbing alcohol)* *(The doctor)* *(BAD)*, and fatty fish eggs popping between teeth *(caviar)*.

I plundered my cache of copied words as we ventured towards an iron door. It loomed taller than two of the other doors stacked atop each other. Glowing red sensors jeweled the exterior. No handle existed on this door.

X-520 marked the outside.

Dame Isobel craned until her eyes were level with two of the red sensors. They flickered, then turned *(yellow)*. Gavin removed a hand-held box from his *(pocket)*. Worms trailed from the box. He jabbed them into the sensor-lights, pushing buttons on the handheld as he did.

One. Two. Three. Three pushes on the middle button.

The worms weren't worms; they were something else that started with a *w* and looked similar.

One. One push on the right button.

Sensors flashed green. *Click.*

The door groaned open.

A glass, water-filled tank dominated the space within—half as large as the cargo hold I'd seen earlier. Submerged and imprisoned in this *(aquarium)*, my skin shivered.

It still resembled my last form. It filled the aquarium to the brim. Sixty-six eyes blinked across the mass of flesh. Seven tentacles flared out, each one thicker than a human thigh. Where they terminated, five smaller tentacles bloomed. Curved hunched top, smooth except where eyes speckled it. The underside bore the ugly rift where they'd ripped it off me. Poor skin. It looked clumsy, slopped on itself in the glass. How easily it would slip through the ocean.

Its membrane threw off rainbow colors in the light.

(*Iridescent*)

What a word. I let it curl up my throat.

"Iridescent," I murmured.

"Fisherman?"

"It looks better than this in the water. My spring-mid-time— it's the form we take when the tubeworms are breeding near the volcanic vents. I have three prehensile tongues you can't see, to suck the worms out and eat them."

How small I am, now.

I stepped towards my skin. It rippled once. Glass quivered.

I took another step—

Dame Isobel's hand clamped down on my shoulder. "We aren't done with the tour yet."

I whipped around, something hot and nasty welling up inside.

"Yessss," I hissed, "We are."

She smiled. Her teeth didn't show, and it didn't change her flat blue eyes. *Unpleasant. Bad.*

"You're my dinner guest," she said.

"No."

I grabbed her wrist. Took her hand off me. Stomped towards my hide.

"Gavin, handle this nicely. Please," Isobel said.

Footsteps lumbered behind me.

The glass was within arm's reach. I touched it—

Something cold stabbed into my neck.

(*needle?*)

Heaviness slammed through my body, increasing with each *pulse* of my single heart. My knees buckled, hitting the floor with a sharp pain. The rest of my followed. Why was the floor touching my face? Metal sucked heat from skin, cold, so cold. Never felt so *cold*. Knees wouldn't function.. Couldn't feel... couldn't.... couldn't stand...

"You'll wake up in time for dinner," Dame Isobel said. "Don't worry. You're my guest until we find the Wishing Fish."

Through numb lips, I slurred, "Wishing—Fish?"

Someone got my shoulders. Gavin. The aquarium receded. Floor slid under me as he dragged my body away from its skin.

Dame Isobel smiled. "You're my very *special guest,* Fisherman. You and I are going to find the Wishing Fish! You don't need that hideous skin-thing now."

"That—that's *me,*" I forced out.

"It's disgusting. You can have it back when we find the Wishing Fish," she said.

The iron door swung shut. *Clunk.*

"You. You promised," I said.

Grey haze filled the room. It blurred her face. Gavin said something into the handheld about getting a weal-chair? (*Wheelchair*)

He glanced at Isobel. "They will be groggy for another hour, then the sedative should wear off."

"Call my guest a *her,* please."

"They don't care what we call them, but *her* is inaccurate."

"Well. It sounds bad. Call the Fisherman a her."

He snorted. "You like that, don't you? Another female. The Fisherman's sleeping in your room, isn't she?"

Isobel went red. Her jaw muscles worked. "What's that supposed to mean, Gavin?"

"They would've hanged you if you were a man. That's what happened to my cousin when they found him out. All I'm saying."

"I'll tell my mother you tried to hurt me," she said quietly.

"She'll believe me over you."

"Because you're a man?"

Gavin's lip curled. "How's the last one doing? Liore, wasn't that her name? Still drooling from the electroshock therapy? Least they didn't execute her like my cousin. Penalty for homosexuality is death, but only the men ever seem to get hanged for it. Women get…. tamed. Poor Liore. She got a lobotomy. You got a ship and a fucking vacation, because you're part of the Dame Family. Second richest family on Europa."

Dame Isobel seethed. "You call *this* a *vacation?*"

"You didn't get your brain destroyed, Isobel."

"I am going to find that alien-god and I am going to make it fix Liore."

"By imprisoning one of its offspring?" he said.

"I'll make it fix her. I can do it."

He pointed at me. "I'll go along with your little quest. I'll do my job, but if you expect me to sit back and watch as you turn this alien *thing* into your newest lover—

"I loved Liore!"

"Not enough to keep them from lobotomizing her."

"You're fired, Gavin. You're fucking fired."

He froze mid-blink. His throat worked.

Then Gavin laughed. "No. I'm not. You don't actually run this ship, Dame Isobel."

Tears streamed down both of Isobel's cheeks. Her chin crinkled like a seabed.

X-520, read the lonely painted label on the door.

I drifted in and out of consciousness as crewmen brought a wheelchair and loaded me onto it. Dame Isobel walked alongside us as they pushed me into an elevator and up to her mansion-quarters. A female crewman threw a blanket over me even though I wasn't cold. The skin of this form wasn't covering enough, apparently. Breast nipples and the moist orifice between my thighs *(vagina) (labia)* were not allowed to be exposed. I had to wear coverings over my covering. Fake skin over skin. Inefficient. I couldn't make it make sense.

"Bizarre. What purpose does your skin serve, then?" I finally asked, yawning.

"Keeps out pathogens and protects our vital organs. Our skin's an organ, too," the female crewman replied.

"It can't change."

"No, not like yours, hon. I can't imagine how bored you are right now," she said.

I sniffled. Snot had filled my nose. Hot water filled my eyes.

"You can't," I sniffled. "You *can't.* Why are my eyes secreting saltwater?"

"You're high on sedatives. Try to sleep."

"I w-want my b-body back," I sobbed.

"You'll get it back when I find the Wishing Fish. If you help me, it might go faster," Isobel said.

"You promised after the tour. You *lied.*"

She smiled again, that nasty, unpleasant smile. "What are you gonna do about it, Fisherman?"

Kill you, I wanted to say.

Kill you, rip out your eyes, steal Gavin's handheld, use both to open X-520, and get my skin.

CHAPTER 3

*D*ame Isobel dined with me alone. Servants put plates of cooked fish and plant matter in front of us, turned, and left. Low, warm lighting suffused from spots along the pale walls. A rectangular table engulfed most of the space. She occupied one end, and I the other. Two candles burned between us, twin fires spuming from their tops. Blue flame. Smelled chemical. Light glittered off Isobel's sand-colored hair and the jeweled flowers pinned atop her head.

Isobel smiled at me. "Would you like wine? It's just the two of us. You can tell me anything, you know. I don't gossip."

"I want my skin," I said.

And then I'd like to dive Home, swim around this ship, grow coils, and drag you all underwater.

"But you're my special guest! You haven't even seen my jewelry collect—"

"Dame Isobel. What do I need to do to get my skin back? What do you want?"

She pouted. Her lips were soft and flushed. Breast tissue spilled over the neckline of her gown. Soft.

I had a sudden urge to touch them.

(*good*)

Warmth filled my belly, though I hadn't eaten. Sweet wetness appeared in the orifice between my thighs. (*good*) (*I want*)

What do those lips taste like?

What does she smell like?

An image: Frilled lips around *her* orifice, swollen with blood, slicked with (*love*)?

Blood rushed down, trailing something akin to electric current.

My pulse thudded down there, now. Throb-throb-throb. The nub of tissue above my orifice tingled.

(*so soft, so good*)

I almost started rubbing my nub to generate more of the good feeling, but had a vague primal feeling that I wasn't supposed to do that in front of another person. Some human social more that kept the species intact. Hm. Interesting. This little nub was a bundle of nerve endings, but what purpose did the pleasure serve? Procreation? I could easily stimulate it at will without ingesting other gametes to produce human young. It was a very cheatable system. How inefficient.

Oh, yes, Dame Isobel. I want to put my mouth on yours. I don't know why.

"Isobel?" I said.

Dame Isobel stared into her wineglass. Her voice dropped. There was a catch in her throat when she spoke.

"The government hurt my friend. I need you to help me find your god, so I can wish for her to get better," she whispered.

"Aeter is asleep. Aeter will be asleep for eons. I can't help you."

"Why should I believe you?"

I picked up my fork and stabbed my portion of whitefish. Tines clinked against the plate.

"Because," I said, stabbing again and again, "If I could get

Aeter to wake up and rescue me, I'd already be gone. This ship—"

Crack!

My plate broke into three shards.

Stupid, breakable things.

I hurled the fork away. It hit the wall tine-first and dug into the wall, quivering. I still felt good and throbbing between my legs, but I also felt hot all over. My jaw clenched.

Dame Isobel blinked. "You're being mean."

(so soft her pupils so soft)

throb-throb-throb.

"Mean? Mean? You ripped my skin off, you—you unchanging little glob of meat and calcium and water," I said, through gritted teeth.

Her mouth, what does it taste like?

So smooth so soft her tongue her candy-pink lips so delicious

"I just wanted you to be comfortable on my ship," she said, licking her lovely lips, not looking at me.

Sweat glistened on her forehead. Her breathing quickened.

"You're...lying. Lying. That's what humans do when they say something that's not true," I said.

"I need to help my friend."

"Your blink rate changed. That's a lie, too."

That sweet spot between my thighs kept throbbing. I tried to ignore it. It served no purpose at this moment.

What do her thighs look like under that silk?

"Fine. Fine, okay, she's not my friend. I love her. I'm not supposed to. They hurt her brain because s-she l-loved me," Isobel said.

"Why is your voice shaking?"

"Please help me."

I stood. I stomped over to her. She remained sitting, curled in on herself.

"They only gave me thirty days to find the Wishing Fish," Isobel said.

"Aeter."

"I'm supposed to get married after that. I only have two weeks left to find the Wishing—Aeter," she said.

"I can't help you. Aeter is a god. Gods wake when they want to. Now, give me my skin. If you do it quickly, maybe I won't destroy this ship," I said.

Throb-throb-throb.

I could smell her, her scent rising: sweat, flower, underneath that something meaty and sweet and tangy—

I want to devour you

But I didn't want to eat her. Wanted to taste. Taste the sweet, silky frilled opening between her—

throb-throb-throb.

Her collarbone, clothed in soft skin. I stroked it between my thumb and forefinger.

Isobel smiled. She leaned back a degree, tongue darting to kiss her lower lip. Saliva shimmered over the coral pink.

I let my hand move down, slipping under the neck of her gown and under another garment. Warmth radiated from her breast. Pores grazed my palm as I pressed. Hairs tickled around the ring of bumps; novae around her nipple.

Oiled glands, those bumps. I could taste it. They secreted a thin hydrophobic salve, lubricating her nipple and areolae, making the skin supple and loveable.

She shuddered a little. She slithered out of her chair, into my touch. She stood.

Silk over my hand, silk-skin underneath. I stroked.

(*I want to devour you*)

Devour. Taste.

A sweet weight settled on my hip. Her thigh. She'd wrapped it around my hip. She curled an arm into me, put her face close to mine. The smell of her filled my nose. Her lips parted as I leaned in, in, face bobbing to hers as if caught in a current…and I put my mouth over hers. Slipped my tongue into her. She tasted of ethanol and *(grape)* and salt; tears she couldn't shed.

(kissing)

Her lips worked against mine. Her orifice ground into my hip, grinding, so sweet, so good, lips wet around it, warm, eager. I clutched a handful of her fine hair. Her slick tongue thrust into my mouth, teasing me. Tastebuds roughened the surface; tasting, she tasted me, I tasted her: *(human) (female) (aroused)*

(sex)

I groped up her thigh, under the gown. Slick lips met my fingers. I slid in, in, thumb arcing up toward a pearl; her nub of nerves crowning the opening.

She made a low, pleasured sound.

I moved my thumb in gentle circles. Smooth, flawless nub. Inside, her muscles contracted around my fingers; she pulsed, pulsed, in rhythmic soundless music. Velvety roof. Delicious motion yes yes, so good, so sweet, yes Isobel—

(!!!!)

It exploded through me—a rush of pleasure and chemicals that annihilated my brain. No thought. No feeling. Only being, in that split-second of love.

She removed her mouth from mine and panted, "Will? You? Help me?"

"Yes," I heard my mouth say.

Yes, to what? Didn't matter. Oozing, dribbling fluids, she contracted with pleasure. Love-chemicals. Hormones.

"We should go. To my quarters. I have a bed. Oh, god. We have to hide it until then. Get off me. Stop smiling, Fisherman."

"Yes."

We managed to hide it until she had us locked back inside her quarters, both of us bleeding, dribbling, and then she lay back and opened her thighs on the bed.

Yes, to what?

My mouth engulfed her sex; delicious, sweet, salty.

Yes, to you, Dame Isobel? I want to go home.

And what would happen to me after two weeks, when Aeter didn't wake, and Dame Isobel had to go home? What would she gift me? An aquarium prison? The other half of her bed? Perhaps even a name besides Fisherman?

Yes, to you, Dame Isobel, you who ripped my skin from my body. You, who cannot exist in my Home. If I dragged you to my quarters, you'd die within seconds.

It sent a bitter not-smile thawing over my face.

Her taste. Her sex.

Those thighs gripped the sides of my face. She occluded everything else. Skin, sweat—surrounded by her, engulfed by her. I gave her pleasure as her hips bucked against my teeth.

Aeter, help me, I prayed.

"Liore," Isobel whispered, "Liore, Liore, Liore, oh god don't stop, Liore."

I was not Liore, so I said nothing.

ISOBEL CUT her arms with a knife when she thought I was sleeping. The ship bobbed gently in Home. Glint-glint, danced the warm light on the delicate blade. Curved, as long as her little finger, the blade quivered. Her hands quivered. Pearl and silver composed the knife handle.

Rocking of the boat.

Blue silk sheets thrown over me, pooling around her hips as she sat up, knife in hand. She pressed the blade to her wrist.

Lush sound, like biting into fresh tubeworm.

(sounds muted by insulating air)

(water conducts; it keeps nothing trapped.)

A dribble of blood oozed down her forearm. Drops hit the sheets and soaked in. Purple stains bloomed.

Her breathing grew heavy, harsh. Tears flowed down her cheeks.

I'm sorry, she mouthed, but I said nothing. She thought I was sleeping. The sheets concealed most of my face.

She made another cut. Shallow slices. Then she scrubbed her bleeding arm over the sheets and blankets, sniffled, and lay down again.

In the night, her arm coiled over me. She stroked my back.

"You have to tell them you're sleeping in the guest room if anyone asks," she murmured. "You can't tell them we're sharing a bed."

"Why?"

"It's illega—it's not allowed. They'll hurt you and me if they find out."

I sat up briskly and swung my legs over the side of the bed. "Oh. I won't do this anymore, then."

"What?"

"You said people would hurt us if they caught us."

Her voice broke. "But—but—"

"If you give me my skin, I won't care. They can do anything they want, and I'd fix it."

"You're being awful."

"I'd be nicer if I had my skin."

"I can't give it to you."

"Why?"

"I'm not really in charge of this ship. Gavin and Anderson would also have to sign off on letting it out…and they won't do it."

"I'm going to be late for migration if you keep me—"

She laughed. A mean laugh. "You heartless fucking alien. I'm bleeding right now. Don't you care?"

I studied her scabbing arms.

"You still have most of your blood inside you," I said helpfully. "It shouldn't matter."

"It does. Oh god, don't go. Don't."

I stood. I padded down the room, towards the doorway.

"I can lock you in the brig, Fisherman."

"What a change that would be," I said.

Two more steps, and I'd be out into the hallway.

"I can starve you. I can strap electrodes to every inch of you and shock you for hours—"

"But you can't make me sleep with you," I said.

I curled up outside the door, in a corner. Cold metal burned my naked skin. I shivered. I tried to grow more hair, then remembered I couldn't. Stupid human skin.

Isobel's footsteps came closer. She stood in the doorway, puffy-eyed. Her white sleeping gown brushed her knees. Nipples poked through the thin material.

A ping through my organs.

(*good*)

Isobel's upper lip curled. "You'll live to regret this."

What was I supposed to say? One minute, she was begging me to touch her, and the next, she was threatening to harm me. Was Isobel brain-damaged? (*crazy*). Something was wrong with her. When things were wrong with someone back Home, Aeter either fixed the issue or ate them. So I'd heard. I'd never seen it myself. It'd happened long before I was created.

"You can't get my skin?" I asked.

She wiped tears away. "Find Aeter for me. The trip ends when we find it."

"It also ends in two weeks. You mentioned you only had two weeks left before your family would send you home."

"Gavin and Anderson won't release your skin. I lied. They know you'll kill us all once you get it back."

My stomach went cold. Invisible ice-water filled it.

"You were never going to let me go, were you?" I said.

She stared at the floor.

Rock-rock-rock, went the boat. Metal creaked. Air percolated.

I'll have to kill those three. Her, Gavin, and Anderson.

Aeter wouldn't be found. I had no other choice.

"I'm sorry," Isobel whispered.

"If I could heal your friend myself, I would say so. And I would do it. I can't. Couldn't even if I had my skin," I said.

"Aeter can."

"Aeter has been sleeping for eons. I'm sorry about your... friend. Is that the word?"

She snorted. "Friend. Yeah. Liore and I were *friends.*"

Aeter, HELP ME.

How she bled. Dame Isobel loved to release her blood.

Blood...

Blood!

Blood carried genetic material and chemicals. If I could bleed, Aeter would taste me. My blood would carry some distress, some of me, chemical stress, and if it got Home—

It could act as a distress call, if Aeter tasted it. Aeter tasted every bit of Home simultaneously. If I could somehow bleed into Home, it might call Aeter.

"Are you dumping your wastewater into Home?" I asked.

"What?"

(ocean) (sea)

I pretended to be more irritated than I was. I felt...cold and small and like I could sleep forever.

She huffed. "You can't just jump from topic to topic like that. We were talking about actual important things, not—"

"Your wastewater's ruining our migration currents. We can taste the used petroleums. Your foreign bacteria. Chemicals. Soaps. Soaps and *shit,*" I said, testing the word as it popped into my thoughts.

"I'm sorry we exist. There. Are you happy?"

"You dump your wastewater right into my home."

"We don't add chemicals or anything, though," Isobel said.

Good. My blood will remain unchanged.

I stood. I headed for the bathroom, brushing past Isobel without a word. She hissed as I did.

Aeter, help me.

I padded into the white stone bathroom. Carved animals leered from under the sink and tub. Baked stone (*ceramic*) surfaces gleamed teal and salt-white.

I put my wrist to my mouth.

I bit.

Hard.

Pain snapped through my skin, hot. It hurt, but I dug deeper with the useless teeth I had, tasting blood. Blood smeared my lips. Blood pearled from the imprint of my teeth and pattered to the sink.

Aeter.

Help me!

I turned the brass faucet and rinsed the blood down the drain.

Landlocked in this foreign skin, would Aeter listen to me? Could Aeter even distinguish my bloods distress from the thousands of other humans bleeding into Home?

These thoughts were inefficient. I ignored them.

Isobel was sitting with her back pressed to the dark wooden headboard when I slinked back to our bed. Her eyes widened when they fell on my wrist.

"You bit yourself?" Isobel asked.

"I'm hungry."

"I can have Celia make you a snack."

I was not actually hungry. I blinked.

"That would be adequate," I said.

She threw the covers back, pouting. One hand crept to the hem of her sleep gown and yanked it up. Glistening vulva lay exposed. Cropped bristles adorned her mons pubis. Hipbones crested on either side of the treasure.

"You can eat me. If you're so hungry," Isobel said.

(*good*)

throb-throb-throb.

"Oh…"

"Eat me, Fisherman."

"That would not be a humorous statement to you if I weren't currently trapped in this pathetic human form," I said.

I swallowed. A burning good thing trailed pretend stars through my innards.

I pressed my lips to her inner thigh. Fresh, slicked flesh. Prickling quivering skin. Bumps roughened as I worked further up, closer, closer. Skin bound over some of her hair follicles; imprisoned in skin, they sat there, curled, behind a translucent wall. How lovely. Rebelling, her skin had formed into red hills around each ingrown hair. A pearl of used dead cells and lymph fluid crowned the top of a hill. I brushed a thumb over it. Smooth. Trapped. A perfect little bead.

Isobel squirmed; it made her sore.

"Your body forms pearls and nodules," I said.

"They're just ingrown hairs."

"I thought you were all useless, frozen things. Now I see. You can change, in little ways."

"You're being silly," she said.

She grabbed my hair. Gently tugged me to her sex. I caressed her labia with my lips, working, tongue gliding over her pearl (*clit*) the pearly-smooth surface of her hard sweet clit, lay-bee-uh, what a sound, her thighs hot and sweaty around me, radiating heat, her smell, her, slicking my chin, getting slippery getting happy, yes taste so (good) Isobel, Isobel—

Her hard feet and legs locked around my shoulders. She strained. Her back arched. Moans came from a deep spot in her throat.

The rhythm: Me, pleasuring her with my tongue, tasting her,

so good; and her, pressing her mutilated arm against the blood-stained sheets, existing briefly in a moment without pain.

THE NEXT MORNING, they imprisoned me in front of a *(mirror)* cabinet box thing *(vanity),* and Isobel acted abnormally. She kept licking her lips. Acidic sweat dampened the underarms of today's gown. Wrinkled Celia, clad in a green smock, ran her fingers through the strands of keratin atop my skull. Hair. My *hair* looked pale, like Isobel's. I'd mimicked Isobel roughly when I formed this body.

Dame Isobel had spent the previous two hours getting twenty-seven different chemicals applied to her facial area. Then another hour during which a scrawny, freckled female brushed cosmetics on. Blue mica powders. Mascara. Kohl liner. Dyed fat for her lips.

Beautiful lips.

So I won't be a monster, she kept saying, with a manic little laugh at the end, and the freckled cosmetic woman stared into her mica powders for a long time.

Now she was ready, but apparently, I was not.

"I want to go home," I said.

Isobel clapped her hands together. "I have a video meeting with my parents! They want to eat breakfast with me! Amazing! They haven't even talked to me since—well, you just sit right here, and let Celia make you look nice."

"I have not eaten in twelve hours except for small bites of your breakfast. I would like to see Home. You call it the ocean," I said.

"Oh, I'm such a silly! Celia! Have your sister send up another breakfast, please."

"I liked the fried cakes with the cubic pattern, the ones you had earlier. You let me have some. I would also like warm tree syrup, please. The curdled animal milk fat was nice. Fatty," I said, "Do you have many of those trees on Earth? The ones full of calorie-rich syrup?"

Celia sighed. Isobel kept smiling. Her smile felt *bad* but not directed at me.

"You heard her, Celia! Well, I'm off. Bye!" Isobel chirped.

She bustled out.

I glanced at Celia. "I would like to see the ocean."

"She's a sweet girl. Means well," she said.

"Yet here I am, trapped."

"Isobel had to watch them do the lobotomy. Her parents made her. It's only been a few weeks since they caught her and her little friend. Please be kind to Isobel."

"Why didn't it happen to Isobel, too? If she did something identical?"

Celia patted my head. "Money."

"What's money?"

"Resources. Food. Security."

"I don't get it."

"She's going through a hard time right now."

"If you get it to me, I won't harm her. I'll take my skin, change, dive back into the ocean, and none of you will ever see me again," I said.

Celia turned away. She went to a little nodule on the wall, pressed it, and spoke. Crackling noises erupted. Then Cherise's voice. Yes, she'd bring the waffles up in thirty minutes. Was the Fisherman thirsty?

"Did she bud to produce you? Is that why you're a genetic clone of Cherise?" I asked.

"Nah. Happened in the womb. It's called being a twin. The sperm fertilizes an egg, but then the fertilized egg splits into two."

"I've observed how unseen you are," I said quietly. "You

could convince Gavin and Anderson to get me my skin. You believe me when I say I won't harm anyone."

She said nothing.

Patterned opalescent paper decorated the walls of this room. Pictorial fish swam beneath waves, eyes bulging as if strangled. I think they were supposed to look eager. In the center of a wall, a half-human, half-fish creature sat perched atop a plant-carpeted rock. Exposed breasts lolled. She clutched a severed human head in one webbed hand. Blood greased her mouth. A milky film blighted her eyes.

Fishermen, native to Europa, read looped ornate writing below the creature in the mural.

Overhead, molded worm creatures snarled along the ceiling.

Prickling started in my scalp. Celia combing my hair.

"It's painful for me to be trapped in one form for this long," I said.

A sharp yank on my hair.

"You'll learn," she said.

"I don't want to be here."

"Isobel needs a friend. Be good to her."

"But—"

"No more. I'm done talking about it," Celia said.

I believed her. I relaxed into my chair. Soft (*velvet*) caressed my palms. The creature in the mural continued smiling. At least someone in this room was happy. She had blood and a head to snack on later.

My stomach made noises. It felt empty inside.

"Such an ugly thing. I keep telling Isobel to have it re-papered or painted over," Celia said, tsking.

"Why is it called a Fisherman?"

For some reason, blood rushed to Celia's face.

"Um. People had ideas. It's just a picture someone painted a long time ago," she said.

"I've never taken that form. I have never seen that form. I

know nobody else who has ever looked like that, and all of us Fisherman know each other."

"Well, nobody really knew what you all were. They had ideas. It's just a picture. Someone painted it a hundred years ago when they first started colonizing Europa. It's just an ugly thing. Don't look at it."

"Is that supposed to be *me?*"

"It's just a picture."

"It's…intriguing," I said. "But inaccurate. We didn't bother ripping off your heads when you came hunting for us. We ate you. All of you. In two swallows."

Celia's throat worked. Her mouth moved soundlessly.

I smiled politely. "But that was a hundred years ago, mostly. Nobody's stupid enough to try capturing us now."

"I—I think I'll put my earbuds in and listen to some music, Fisherman. While I style your hair."

"That is adequate."

Hands trembling, she fished two small white earpieces from her pocket, inserted them, and sounds murmured out. *Yank-yank-yank* went the comb in my hair. I wanted to ask her to cut it off, because my hair was annoying, but she seemed very preoccupied.

She slicked jelly into my hair. She pinned it into a coil at the base of my neck, sliding in a jeweled comb. The gemstones felt cold under my fingers as I probed.

Cherise came in, left my food, and departed.

Celia told me to eat before she laced me into my gown. Yes, I was supposed to wear a gown. In fact, it was one of Isobel's gowns. It would be better to avoid staining the silk by eating beforehand…

Aeter, O creator and parent, help me.

I had just put my fork into a fried cake when Isobel burst in, tears streaming down her face.

She wailed, "They're making me marry him!"

Celia hurried over, taking her wrists in hand. "Who? What's going on, Isobel? Take a breath. Tell me."

"They're making me marry Gariellus Paloma. The wedding preparations start in three weeks. I have to go—"

A sob.

"I—I have to be home in Brilliante in three weeks. I only have three weeks to find the god-thing and m-make it f-fix Liore, and I can't find it, and after I marry Paloma—he won't let me go looking, he can't, couldn't even if he wanted to. I'm supposed to socialize. Coordinate. All the shit my mother does—"

"Paloma's sweet on you. Why wouldn't he get Liore some advanced medical treatment for the brain damage?"

"There's nothing that can help her."

"How do you know?"

Isobel took her thin shoe off. She hurled it at the wall. It hit the mural creature between the eyes and bounced.

"You think if there was something that could help her, I couldn't've found it? Afforded it? You think my parents wouldn't have tried fixing her? They liked Liore. Well. When they thought she was just *my friend*, right?"

Isobel made a horrible keening noise that dissolved into sobs. "I c-can't live like this, knowing I'm fine and she's drooling in a fucking chair because we got caught. I knew she was poor. I knew they could haul you to one of those places and let the doctors do it—"

"You tried."

"She was smart. She wanted to go back to college, get a bioengineering degree. Now we're lucky if she can remember what she ate for breakfast."

"Isobel—"

"I hate this fucking place."

Dame Isobel leaned against the vanity as if shot. Her

knuckles went white as she gripped. Vacant-eyed, she put her left pinky in her mouth and sucked on it.

"But. We'll have a nice lunch with the crewmen. I have three weeks left. I'll find Aeter, the Wishing Fish, and it will fix Liore. Get the Fisherman ready for lunch, please," she said.

"I'm sorry about your friend," I said.

"Don't be. She'll get better soon," and the smile that spread across Isobel's face was so crazed it sent a wave of revulsion through my guts.

CHAPTER 4

*R*ed-eyed, still teary, Isobel showed me the portrait of her parents before she turned on our video chat.

Dame Serena, mother. Dame Jux, father. Intricate bone-white braids haloed Serena's skull. In the picture, she smiled stiffly, posture unnatural. Rows of gold rings enclosed both eyebrows. Exposed nostrils looked like twin black slits above her nose—botched surgery, Isobel said. Behind Serena, Dame Jux had his hand draped over her shoulder; a meatless man, his cheekbones strained his wrinkled skin. Fingers like sea-spiders *(tasty)*. His hair had gone silver from age.

They were colorless people, the two of them. Bleached. It made their blue silk garments glow in comparison.

"He's much older than her," I said helpfully.

Isobel pressed a button on the glass video screen. "Don't say that in front of them."

"That doesn't make sense. Human couplings should be similar in age for maximum fecundity. Your mother wasted fertile years on this male."

"Oh my god, you're a fertility expert now?"

"You aren't supposed to copulate based on feelings, so says

this culture. According to you. I can only assume the basis for copulation is reproductive potential."

"When you're rich, it's about money."

"How does copulating with an aging male create money?"

The video screen crackled.

Isobel's mother materialized on the viewing screen. Old. She looked so very weak, denuded of cosmetics and jewelry. She lay in bed, head propped on pillows. Her loose bone-colored hair fanned over the pillows. Dim blue lighting shadowed her features, radiation through a phosphor, unnatural lighting for humans.

Alien. She looked like something I'd find in a trench.

Her voice had teeth. Brittle and sharp. "Isobel. Who's your friend?"

"I'm not marrying Paloma," Isobel said.

"Don't make us sedate you."

Isobel stiffened. "He won't want to fuck me if I'm drugged—"

"Who's your new friend?"

"It's not like that. I caught one of the Fishermen, and she changed into human for me. She and I are discussing trade opportunities—"

"We never could teach you to lie well. No matter how many instructors we paid, " Serena said.

"Paloma doesn't care what I do. As long as he gets to stick it in me."

"We can't afford another scandal."

Here's a chance to get my skin.

"Dame Serena," I said, "I'm being held here against my will, and they've taken my skin so I can't return home. If you get them to return my skin, I'll lead you to a vein of precious metals hidden in a trench."

Isobel hissed. She whipped around to face me.

"Against your will? *Against your will?* It didn't seem that way last night—"

"Quiet," Serena snapped. "Fisherman, can you hear me?"

"Yes, Dame Serena."

"I can't let you go. You'd be free to ruin the Dame family's reputation. I apologize for my daughter's actions, but I can't set you free."

My heart started beating in my stomach. Impossible. My throat went dry.

"You can," I said.

"I can and I can't. The Dame family supports hundreds of thousands of people. If we collapse, so do they."

throb-throb-throb.

"How would that make you collapse?" I asked.

"Scandal."

"What does that word mean?"

Serena made a raspy, crackling noise.

I seized Isobel by the throat, jammed my other hand over her mouth so she couldn't scream, and pinned her in her chair. I clambered atop her. She struggled. I held.

Calm, I turned back to the video screen. Isobel's tongue lashed against my palm, tickling.

"Is it impossible now, Dame Serena?" I asked.

More cackling. Her lungs did not function well.

"Oh," she said between laughs, "Please do. Isobel's better to us dead than alive. If she's dead, it means a televised funeral and Europa's sympathy. Alive, she's a walking, talking scandal. A para-site. Please, do what none of us had the stomach to do. Kill Isobel."

Isobel went limp.

"Would you return my skin if I did?" I asked.

A flicker of something. Dread. I did not want to end Isobel's life. Interesting.

"No. But I'd keep you in luxury. You could have anything you wanted, besides freedom. Consider it payment."

"I will not kill your daughter for human trifles."

"Suit yourself," Serena said. "Isobel. If you want to live beyond the next six months, you're going to do three things. One, marry Paloma. Two, stop screwing women."

I released Isobel. I stepped back. She shivered and curled into a fetal position.

"You should like the last one. It involves you being a celebrity," Serena said.

Isobel said nothing. She didn't look capable of it.

"You're going to be the new public face of LUV."

Isobel shook her head.

"Oh, yes. Francine sent over the paperwork. You had a long stay there, you see. A very public stay. We've already generated and circulated the pictures of you in the facility, going to change therapy, healing your sexuality. Poor Liore Hyung would've been saved if she'd applied through LUV's public charity program," Serena said. "I might even actually send you there if you keep causing scandals."

"Lobotomize the women, hang the men," I said.

"As a last resort," Serena said.

"Why? Why the difference? What sense does any of this make?" I asked.

Blue light glinted off her wet teeth.

"You have paperwork to do, Isobel," Serena said.

The video screen went black.

We had to converse with crewmen in less than thirty minutes. I nudged Isobel. She blinked, reanimating. Shock tinged her sweat, metallic and rank.

She shook her head. "Kill me. I can't live. Not here."

"Do you…is there another place you can live?"

"There's nowhere I can go without being Dame Isobel," she said, so softly.

I had no good words. I kissed her, slowly, and she nestled into me. When she sobbed, I didn't push her away. My chest got messy from her tears and mucus, but I did not push her away. I should've.

Somehow, I couldn't.

❧

THREE DAYS. One. Two. Three.

Three bite marks on my arms.

Mine.

Dame Isobel let me outside three times, once a day. After the crew ate—I always smelled the faux soy-meat on their breath when they entered the passcode to her chamber. Blue silk concealed the metal walls. I couldn't stop clawing 'skin' off my arms, bleeding, licking to taste the salt.

My skin pulsed four levels below me in its aquarium.

"What the hell is it, anyway?"

"Her new pet. I think she fucks it. I don't know."

"No, not that. It was a ball of meat on the deck three days ago. What is it?"

A pause.

"First job assignment on Europa?"

"Yeah."

"It's a Fisherman. They're native here—keep to themselves, mostly."

They opened the door. "Hands out."

Two crew mates, both males. I held out my wrists, and they cuffed me.

"Is it a woman?"

The older one snorted. "Don't get any ideas. Dame Isobel doesn't share her toys."

We walked down the ship corridor.

A quick glance at me. Light haloed the younger male's hair.

"We could report Isobel for it," he said softly. "This is her second offense. It's got a woman's body, they're gonna care about—"

"You don't make allegations like that against the Dame family, Aaron," the old human said. "Just because your brother's the captain doesn't mean you can get cocky."

"They got her first offense, didn't they?"

I shut my eyes, trying to concentrate—*spikes, something sharp, slice them open*—and failed. Nothing formed.

Through gritted teeth, "Liore Hyung was a human being. Not a first offense," the old human said.

They led me through a sea of metal-plated corridors until we arrived at the observation deck. Thick glass encased any exit.

"Fifteen minutes. Don't touch the glass," the old human said.

I grunted. He nodded. Waves rocked the boat, ever-so-slightly, like unseen gravity. Engines droned. Water roiled beneath the ice. Black sky limned the ice plates. Jove tugged overhead, as always, a creamy blot covering half the darkness. Nothing else lived above the ice, lifeless as flat human skin.

Aaron scuffed his boots and stared. Grime caked his clothing. Clothing. Ugh. More like dead fabric strangling useless flesh that couldn't adapt to temperatures.

"I don't like it," he said.

"Can't do anything to hurt us. Don't you know how Fishermen work?"

"I don't even know what *it is*."

Old human scrubbed a hand over his white stubble. Fish-belly pale skin lay furrowed over his face and sagged on his blighted hands. "All right. They shapeshift to meet the needs of their environment. Jupiter throws off so much radiation that they've got to. There's hardly any light. Only heat. Not a hell of a lot of living matter to consume. I knew one. Said they could live off radiation in one of their forms. That sort of thing."

"They can talk?"

"They're intelligent."

Aaron scoffed. "Where's civilization, then? Didn't have shit until we started colonizing a hundred years ago."

"They don't need to build civilization to live. They morph to fit the environment. This one isn't doing it because Dame Isobel ripped off the thing that lets it shapeshift," the old human said.

"Yes," I said, "I need to go home. I can't go home without my skin."

"E.T., phone home," Aaron said, snorting.

"E.T.?"

"Ah, quit being a dickhead, Aaron."

"My genetic layer—my skin. I can't leave without it. If you'd like me gone, bring me my skin. It's in a locked tank below us."

Aaron's face reddened. "Wait. Dame Isobel's basically holding a—a person captive? And she's fucking it. It. Her. Her?"

"Six minutes left, Fisherman," old human said.

I should probably ask the old human his name. He'd think better of me. I could manipulate him more easily. Yes.

"What's your name?" I asked the old human.

"Five minutes, thirty seconds, Fisherman."

"You're humans. You like seabed metals. Retrieve my skin, and I'll show you where some are. I'll make you wealthier than the Dame family could ever dream of being…there are hidden veins of metal you'll never find without me," I said.

Aaron goggled at me.

The ship shuddered.

Impact hit. Force. It knocked me down.

SCRREEEK!

"Shit!" the old crewman snarled.

Both men jumped to their feet, panting. Noise crackled out of their ears.

"What did we—"

"Something alive. Saying we hit something native—"

The ship floor canted.

The others found me. They stopped their migration to look for me, and now they're here to rescue me! I can go HOME!

I smiled so hard my face hurt.

Then blackness engulfed my vision.

Silence.

Out of the black void, came an amused gurgle.

They're calling me the Wishing Fish?

I tried to speak, but I had no mouth. I knew the voice. I'd never felt it before, but I knew it, deep in some atavistic node of my body.

Aeter.

They responded. *Yes.*

Have you come to grow me another skin, Aeter?

Another gurgle.

Aren't you bold? Aeter said.

TAPPING ON MY CHEEK.

"Wake up."

Aeter?

The old human stood over me, lips moving. Harsh light haloed his head.

"Up you get. Dame Isobel needs you at the bow of the ship," he said.

Once again, Dame Isobel *needed something.*

Heat flared through my chest. "I'll come."

"We hit something alive. She wants you to communicate with it."

I prayed, *Crush this ship, Aeter.*

Aeter said, *I'm not going to crush the ship for you, Little One. This is...fascinating.*

Crewmen herded me. When we arrived at the bow, Dame Isobel gestured for the crewmen to leave, and they filed out.

The two of us stood alone.

"It's the Wishing Fish, isn't it?" Isobel breathed. "Aeter. The Dreaming Impulse—"

"Don't say that out loud."

The boat vibrated softly, stopped, and started again. Rhythmic motion. Dame Isobel rubbed her face.

It's been a few eons since I breathed, Aeter said.

Isobel's eyes were too bright. She licked her lips. "Talk to it."

"I am."

"What? Then ask for something! Ask for it to heal Liore!"

More heat built in my guts. Hm. Why? Was this a biochemical 'emotion'?

"You don't ask the Dreaming Impulse for things. They give as They choose," I said.

Blood soaked through Isobel's blue silk sleeve. She'd been cutting herself again.

"Wish for something," Isobel said.

"What's a 'wish'?" I asked, digging my nails into my palms.

"It's something you want, but don't have."

"You want a lot," I said.

She sniffled. "I—I just want someone to help Liore, and then I want to find someone who loves me. Don't you love me?"

"Not particularly, Isobel."

"You're so silly, Fisherman. I know you try, but you don't understand anything. They'll kill or maim anyone I ever love. Paloma means well, and he tries...but I'm Dame Isobel, and I can't escape that. Even if I never got married, I'd be...."

A shrill noise came out of her. "Y-you know. Gay. They do things to gays. They made me watch an execution when I was twelve. They hanged a man by the docks and he kept seizing on the rope and they made me watch while he—while he died."

"Died?"

"Stopped existing. Dead."

I padded over to the railing, a slab of waist-high metal.

Airtight glass imprisoned overhead. Vents whined as they circulated too-hot air. My current skin tolerated it, but it felt wrong. An unnatural heat. I stared up at Jove.

I said, *Aeter, I despise Dame Isobel, but she is trapped in terrible circumstances. You know I can't adapt without my skin. I'm stuck.*

Broken ice-plates shifted below. Something massive rolled under the ice.

Are you? Aeter said.

They sent me a mental picture. Dame Isobel, lying on the floor in a puddle of blood, not breathing, amid a thick reek of fecal matter. Died? Was this 'dead'?

She's been looking for you...something about wishes? I thought.

The boat jolted.

Is she? Would you ask that of Me?

Ice plates crashed into each other. Broke. I swallowed. *All I want is my skin. All I want is to return home, Aeter.*

You'll have to adapt, Aeter said.

Energy boiled up my throat, a long harsh scream I clamped my lips around—

I CAN'T!

"What's happening with Aeter?" Dame Isobel asked.

Did she ever shut up?

"Aeter's decided to grant your wishes. All of them," I snapped.

She paled.

My creator and parent, asleep for eons, had woken to commune with me. My blood might've triggered Them to wake. Dame Isobel wanted me to tell Aeter, god of the eternal ocean, to grant her petty wishes. Stupid human Isobel. I could not begrudge her humanity or desperation; she suffered. She did not fit in, but—

She took MY SKIN, Aeter!

I exhaled through my clenched teeth. Angry. This was anger.

How did I create matter? Tell me. How did I bring it into being? Aeter said. They hadn't liquified me yet. They weren't angry.

How had Aeter created us? Through *(dreams)*. Dreams, slicked into matter as they gestated in Aeter's body, a spinning gyre of protein and flesh, ever-changing, reabsorbed and turned into new life. Incubated, like the petri dishes of bacteria in the ship's lab.

But I can't. Not like you.

Dame Isobel clutched my arm. "Tell the Wishing Fish to heal Liore Hyung. And to kill Gariellus Paloma. I can't marry him."

I smiled, nodded. I was puzzling over the divine riddle.

Done, Aeter said.

"What's Aeter saying?"

"Yes," I said.

See what happens, Aeter thought. The ice shifted one last time before stilling. *Call out to me. I'll be listening.*

"Thank you," Isobel said.

Her pupils bloomed, softened. Barely any of her blue iris peeked out. She kissed my neck. Pleasure zinged down, prickling my skin.

"Let's go back to our room," she said. "Let's make love."

Oh. Oh, oh.

HORMONES RANG IN OUR SWEAT—HUMAN chemical impulse wrought into being. Invisible electricity, building heat. Taste of sex. Salty, like home. Like tears. I lapped at her sex while her hips thrusted, bucked. Held her still, listened to her moans, the frantic pace of her breaths and something *(soft)* and *(sweet)* rustled in me and coiled. Rush of stickiness trickled between my thighs.

Her nub of nerves, the hood of flesh. Oh yes.

Her, panting.

Yes, yes.

She wanted to do it to me after she came, but I shook my head. "I'm sleepy."

I actually wanted to speak to Aeter without distraction, but the lie was adequate.

"You think Aeter's granted my wish already?"

"Mm."

Pound! Pound! Pound!

Isobel went taut, upper lip curling.

"I said not to bother me!" she screamed.

The door remained closed. The crewman's voice was calm and emotionless. How had he gotten past Celia? Celia normally would be fetching Isobel. Something was wrong. Celia was supposed to be working right now.

"What happened to Celia?" I asked.

"Dame Isobel. Ma'am. The crew's having…difficulties."

Isobel rolled her eyes. She waved a hand at the wall, yanked on a silk robe, and padded to the door.

The wall lit up pink. An ad for something called a "Real-Doll," played. A muscular male caressed a silicon simulacrum shaped like a female. "…a partner that never gets a headache, amiright? Customize her appearance for no additional charge! Now with realistic vaginal movement during play!"

Change for me. You're a Fisherman. Lick me down there. Make love to me. Do what I want—

I started crying as the ad ended. I didn't know why.

Dame Isobel tasted fine, of salt—*of home I want to go HOME* —and the microbiota in her fluids tingled faintly in my mouth. To taste. Oh, to taste. If we did this when I had my skin, I could sing the genetics of her.

Dame Isobel flicked her finger at the wall, not looking. Channels changed. The news channel blared. I didn't move from the bed. I nestled into the silk sheets, wiping away tears.

What makes your coitus so wrong? She's the alien here, Aeter murmured, *have her wish for something better. Or kill her.*

Isobel stood at the door, hands on hips. "The crew's paid well. Go bother the captain."

"Ma'am…the captain's the one encouraging it."

"The Dame family doesn't take kindly to mutiny," Isobel said. "We're only here for two more weeks. We found the Wishing Fish. What, do they want more pay? I can arrange that. I can—"

"It's your Fisherman. Some of the, uh, crewmen don't like it."

"It's helping us communicate with the Wishing Fish. It stays."

A long silence, broken only by low-volume news announcements.

"Ma'am, with all due respect, we found the entity. It's gone. It swam away. The crewmen want to go home."

Dame Isobel stood.

"Ma'am? Are you there?"

"Yes. Yes, I'm here. I'll bump up everyone's pay by 20%, effective immediately. Go inform the captain. He can handle the paystubs. Or he can find whoever does—just go. Please. The Fisherman stays, and that's final."

"I tried to warn you. Remember that."

"Go."

Footsteps retreated.

Dame Isobel embraced me until I couldn't breathe. Her nipples stiffened through the silk robe.

"I love you," she whispered against my ear, "No matter what anyone else says. Love me."

"Right now? Again?"

She dragged me over to the bed.

"Will you give me my skin back if I do?"

"Of course, dear," she said, and laughed.

It was the fifth time in a row we'd had that exchange. It amused her every time.

Spikes. Grow bones, something sharp.

During coitus.

A shard of warmth bloomed on my wrists, heat beneath skin, and Aeter the Dreaming Impulse murmured to me, far below the endless ocean.

How long will you let them hurt you? Adapt, Little One.

Isobel and I migrated to our designated beds. We slept.

In the morning, Celia woke us each individually, frowning as if she smelled something foul.

"You shouldn't be alone with your…friend, Isobel," she muttered.

"Oh, please. She won't hurt me. Can't get what she wants if she does," Isobel said.

"Just the same, bring LaBeouf along," Celia said.

LaBeouf?

Gavin LaBeouf.

Dame Isobel let me follow along as she completed daily tasks, most of which involved sitting for her three-hour beauty routine, talking into video screens, smiling at intervals—a smile that did not reach her eyes—and inquiring about financial matters. I read books about Earth, ones swollen with pictures of flora and fauna, smiling to myself. I glutted on knowledge. People here gave it so freely.

If Celia wasn't with us, Gavin was. He never said anything. He watched from behind, dark eyes charting every movement I made.

At one point, Isobel slinked down to a dimly lit room with special blue lights staged around it. She slid several pearl bracelets up her wrists and contorted her body into sensual poses. Embedded cameras snapped pictures. *Influencing,* Isobel called it. A jewelry company had paid her to pose with their bracelets. Apparently, that made people want to buy them more. What difference did it make whether they had staged pictures of Isobel wearing them? Why?

Stupid.

"It's a waste of two hours," I said. "You derive no enjoyment from this activity. It serves no purpose. You could be learning something, experimenting with a philosophy, or constructing mental concepts for others to enjoy."

"I'm the Jewel of Europa. I make tons of money doing this," she said.

"But why?"

She snorted. "Because people are stupid, and they like pretty things. Hah. They think they're me if they buy the bracelets, deep down. It makes all the dirty, disgusting miners and dish-washers and sewage workers feel like there's something beau-tiful to fight for."

"Beauty?"

She pointed to me. In the blue lighting, her face looked alien. "You wouldn't know, Fisherman. You're a shapeshifting monster-thing."

"Oh."

"But I mean, you're not that bad right now. Except your face. Your mouth and nose are all twisted, but it's cute."

"I lacked the time to mimic you perfectly."

Because you ripped my skin off.

Blood burned through my face, radiating heat.

You peeled my skin OFF.

Gavin cleared his throat. "Isobel, you have a meeting in seven minutes. Should I escort the Fisherman back to her room?"

"You think that's necessary, Gavin?"

"She looks tired."

I clenched my fists. "I'm not."

Isobel turned, scanned me, pursed her lips. They made a juicy o shape. Mesmerizing. Her breasts hung against the thin silk of her gown.

"Yeah..." she said slowly. "Fisherman, go read some books in your room. Someone'll get you for lunch in an hour."

Gavin escorted me. I went. I said nothing.

After lunch, Dame Isobel clutched her hands together in her lap until the blood left her knuckles. She pressed the call button for Celia.

"Celia, please put Paloma on. We're supposed to talk in ten minutes. I won't be the late one," Dame Isobel said.

She gnawed her lip. Her beautiful lip. A bit of skin stuck out. She ripped it off. Blood pearled from the raw, exposed layer beneath.

I kissed it off. Licked. Delicious. Salty. Tasted like Isobel, like her hormones and skin cells.

Dame Isobel stiffened. "Is Celia here? Did she see?"

"Nobody's here but us."

"You have to be more careful than that," she said, shaking her head. "Gavin's okay, but nobody else can see us. If someone besides Gavin sees us, they'll hurt *you*. Not me. Please. I can't—I can't have another Liore."

"Your mother said she wanted to kill you."

"She'll hurt you before she hurts me."

Someone rapped on the door.

"Isobel?" Celia called.

Isobel untangled herself from me and wiped her mouth on the back of her hand. "Come in."

"Paloma's sick. He isn't available to talk," Celia said.

"Sick?"

"Yes, dear. Do you still want to have lunch with the crew? Do you need to cry for a bit?"

Isobel grinned. Unpleasantly.

"I'll manage," she said, leaning in to kiss me.

AETER WAS VAGUELY surprised that we had not exterminated the human infestation. Only the ones who'd directly harmed or attempted to harm us.

We were waiting for you to wake up, I explained.

Stupid, Aeter said, *Are you all this passive, my Little Ones? Did I not give you the capacity to defend yourselves?*

Here I sighed. *The humans only use the surface, where we seldom go. Why bother? What purpose does destroying harmless living creatures serve?*

Aeter said, *Harmless?*

They've never stolen one of our skins before—

That you know of.

They're sentient and capable of feeling pain, I thought.

Aeter peered through my eyes into emptying lunchroom, littered in human flotsam: balls of aluminum foil smeared in oleaginous condiment, chipped red plastic tables, dirty plastic trays, waxed gum wrappers, murmurs, clattering silverware, stench of artificial meat and barbeque sauce and sickly sweet chemical cleaner, coughs, orange-jump suited crewmen filing out of the doors, wet blue-striped rags festering on the tables, clotted with diluted cleaner, bleak wall-mounted clock looming over all, numerals cold electric blue, Dame Isobel's tight grip on my forearm.

Aeter said, *Do you care about them and their lives?*

I had no answer.

If you do, tell me, They said. *If you all enjoy the diversion of having other lifeforms here, that's fine. But remember. You were here first. If you don't like the human society they've constructed, fix it. You are all powerful enough on your own to rebuild their society. I won't do everything for you, Little One.*

"I'm not miserable," I lied.

Dame Isobel made a soft sound and gripped my arm tighter.

Aeter's voice grew loud enough to make my eardrums burn.

"Every time you have intercourse with her, or touch her, you're reinforcing a biochemical bond between the two of you.

That's how human intercourse works. Are you aware of this?" Aeter said.

"....yes..." I said.

"It's influencing your decisions."

I thought, *Then solve the issue. Grow me a new skin. I'll leave.*

Aeter laughed in Their gurgling way. Isobel smiled at me. Silly Fisherman, her expression said. Aeter was amused. Isobel was amused. Not a single person moved to clean the scattered trash in the lunchroom—they couldn't even deign to throw it in the designated receptacles. I huffed. I moved to pick up a gum wrapper, but Isobel tugged my elbow.

"No, no. We pay people to do that," she said.

"Someone needs to clean up the mess," I snapped.

My face burned. Something invisible constricted my chest, made my throat ache. The beginnings of tears tingled through my nasal area.

I am feeling a disproportionate emotion. Why?

"Someone—" my voice broke. "Someone should do something."

"Fisherman?"

"Because living creatures are suffering. The litter. It is unsightly and will breed harmful pathogens," I said. "Look what they made. Look at it. It—"

Tears filled my eyes. I blinked them away.

She gave a laugh. "It's just trash. Come on. I need your opinion on the ballroom decor."

Somehow, everyone was amused except me.

CHAPTER 5

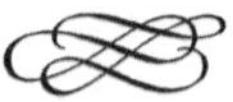

*B*ecause Isobel never bothered asking me, and Liore didn't know to ask, I'll tell you directly. For your understanding.

Knowledge is our currency.

Europa's sterile oceans stretch for aeons before you find other life. There's a reason most of our forms feed on radiation instead of flesh. We live solitary lives, except for brief migratory periods, during which knowledge trading occurs. Stories, concepts, questions, facts—valued in that order. Questions asked, left to unspool in your mind. What better to keep you occupied?

I wondered if anyone else cared that I'd miss migration. Would they track down the ENS *Princess*? Conduct a rescue mission? Hopeful thoughts. Mostly likely, they wouldn't. I had a very close Friend, My Friend, that I was supposed to meet with before migration. We were supposed to migrate side-by-side. My Friend. They always chided me for being slow, for being too passive and introspective. *Look at the tubeworms! Watch me draw a story on the seabed. Finish the story. Give it a new ending. Surprise me,* My Friend would say, but I'd always tell them, *You finish it. It's your concept.*

Both of us knew that wasn't the truth. My Friend didn't probe further.

What's the point? This serves no purpose, I wanted to say, *All of this playing.*

Now I regretted every single time I'd said that.

At night, I cried. I dreamed about My Friend. I dreamed about the others coming to rescue me from this terrible place—shapes crowding the prison ship, coiling around, dragging it under, prying that aquarium open, releasing my skin, to be freed, to be home—

Useless dreams. Everyone would assume I was handling other affairs or reproducing. My Friend was the only one that might notice my absence, and if they did, they'd assume I had a reason for being gone.

So.

Knowledge is value.

Concepts, philosophy, knowledge, stories—everyone on the ENS *Princess* sloshed it out, gave up their stories, like throwing handfuls of sapphires around. I was greedy for knowledge. That was partly why I didn't make more effort to reclaim my skin.

(The others would gape at me if they found out how freely I'm giving you this very tale. Glutted on blood and entrails as I am right now, I'm feeling benevolent.)

"WE COULD HAVE A PARTY, maybe. To stop the crew from mutinying. Fisherman, what do you think?"

A party:

Blue silk. Human moving, dancing; swirling bodies in unseen currents. Silver ribbons, composed of real metals, festooning the walls. Taste of sweet grape, distorted by fermentation, burning down my throat. Warm mouth from smiling, sore throat from talking. Crystal glasses thin-stemmed as optic nerves, shivering on trays carried by blurry-faced black-clad humans; (*servers*), and they aren't blurry-faced. Isobel can't remember their faces, she never looked. Glimmering plastic. Synthetic gowns. Dancing, heels clicking on stone floors; click-click, laughing, liquid sounds, a constant stream of noise. A smell of sweat, fake flowers, cooked spiced flesh.

Those memories flashed through my brain when Isobel mentioned having a party. We ate breakfast in bed. She'd dripped coffee all over the silk sheets, but didn't seem to care.

"What's wrong with the crew?"

"Oh, they don't like you very much."

"Return my skin and let me leave the ship. That would solve the issue more efficiently than this 'party' idea," I said.

"Don't be a party pooper. I want to have a party! We'll have the party," Dame Isobel said, beaming.

Coral dye coated her lush lips. Honey and champagne sweetened her breath. She speared a bite of honey-glazed bun and took another sip of coffee. Alcohol and caffeine. Depressant and a stimulant. Could that damage her?

"Isobel, I've never seen you drink alcohol this quickly after waking," I said.

"It's nothing! Just having fun. I need to relax. Okay?"

"I don't think it's healthy to chemically lobotomize yourself," I said.

She rolled her eyes and took a long, lurid glug of champagne.

I'd tried wine once. Hated it. Why would anyone willingly cloud their mind?

Since Aeter wouldn't rescue me, I needed to get Gavin's handheld and convince Isobel to stare at the door of X-520 until it unlocked. I could liberate my skin then.

And leave Isobel to suffer?

My stomach suddenly hurt.

"Will Gavin be monitoring conduct at this party? When and where? Where does he live when he isn't working?" I asked.

She waved a manicured hand. "Oh, he'll handle it. He always does."

"Shouldn't we ensure that he understands the...purpose of this party? I think he'll be more motivated if I can convince him that it'll reduce the possibility of physical conflict or mutiny," I said.

"I didn't think you'd care," Isobel said, blinking. "I thought you'd say it sounded inefficient, inadequate, and human."

"If it will make you happy, my life will be—"

"You won't persuade him to give you your skin," Isobel said.

My stomach clenched.

"I was raised around liars, Fisherman. You're not good at it. Why do you really want to see Gavin?"

I could tell her. She might even take my side. Possibly. Of course, she could get offended and imprison me in the steel brig, where I'd have no chance at escape. Even if I managed to steal Gavin's handheld, I'd have still to convince Isobel to unlock the door via retinal scan. Or carve her eyes out. What a plan. To make Isobel's life worse, imprison her more, by stealing her eyesight. Terrible plan. It was efficient, but the thought of hurting Isobel made me feel cold and small. I couldn't do it. No chance.

Small chance versus no chance.

I am a logical creature, despite what the news channels say.

I stared her directly in the eye. "I want to steal Gavin's handheld thing, the one that unlocks X-520, so I can get my skin. Then I'll have you look at the door for the other locks. Then I will go home. You found Aeter. Let me go home."

She flinched as if I'd slapped her. Her lip wobbled. "All this time, and you still want to leave me?"

"Isobel. I am not human. I do not want to live the rest of my existence pretending to be. It has nothing to do with you," I said.

"Kill me."

"What?"

"I'll get you that fucking e-key of Gavin's," she said, eyes brightening, voice going horribly soft, "In exchange for taking the bioplastic wires out of my arms. My parents had them surgically implanted after I tried the first time. I was twelve. I have a tox filter implanted in my stomach, and titanium mesh between my dura mater and skull. So, I can't put a bullet through it. Nobody gets to kill themselves in the Dame family."

"How was your mother planning on killing you, then?" I said.

"Electric shock. That's the usual."

"I'm sorry your existence hurts."

She reached under her skirts. A leather sheath was strapped to her thigh. She drew her cutting knife.

Quick as thought, Isobel slashed her forearm open. Wrist to elbow. Her facial expression remained neutral. Blood spurted. White tendons poked out from the slice. Red muscle glistened.

A peek of blue curled out, unfurling.

Blood puddled the floor, gushing, smell thick enough to taste. That didn't seem good. How much blood did humans have? Why couldn't I move? Why was my stupid body so stiff? Vomit tickled the back of my throat.

Blue wires exploded over the wound. They meshed, weaving into a net. The blood flow halted. Isobel's ruined arm looked as if she wore a lacy, blue-veined glove, or a long sleeve.

From a distance, you couldn't see how badly she hurt.

"They'll turn skin-colored after fifteen minutes," she said.

"You want me to remove those from your arms?"

"Uproot them."

Isobel ran the knife over the mesh. It held.

"They're cut-proof," she said.

"What happens after I do?" I asked.

She blinked twice. She rubbed her eyes on the back of her hand.

"I leave. For good. I go to sleep and never wake up," she said.

That was a lie. She would bleed out and her existence would cease.

"No," I said.

"How badly do you want to escape?"

"Enough to kill."

"But not me? That's where you draw the fucking line? You won't let me kill myself?" Isobel said.

"I am very aware of how illogical that is."

"I'll get you that e-key. We'll do it this afternoon. After I video-chat with Liore."

Her mouth twisted. "LUV is having me do a live interview tonight."

"Why does that disturb you?"

"They want me to say things that hurt other people. I'm supposed to pretend that I went to one of their facilities, had therapy, and came back attracted to males. That I'm not—you know, into women."

"I see. You're giving away an idea-philosophy-theory—I can't describe what I'm trying to—"

I spat out a few curse words. Cleanse the mouth. It felt good.

"Do you get other knowledge in exchange for selling that idea?"

"I get money," she said bitterly.

"Someone kept peddling a bad philosophy, once. It was like a virus. A lot of us started bashing ourselves against rock shelves. Not me. I still don't know what it was. It had to be tempered with other mental concepts to make them stop."

"I'm going to be gone before that interview. Doesn't matter."

"It's a live interview," I said.

"So?"

"They can't edit what you say."

"I can't fight. I'm done."

"You sound like me," I said.

Was this what Aeter meant? When They called me passive?

"I found Aeter. I did everything I cared about. Fuck the party. Fuck the crew and their mutiny, fuck it—"

"Does anyone know what they did to Liore?" I asked.

Isobel's jaw worked. "What does it matter?"

"How would people react if they knew Liore was lobotomized because of LUV's ideology?"

"People know."

"Do they?"

"I can't do anything. Stop asking. Be here at two. I'll have the e-key for you," Isobel said.

She waved at the door.

I tried to speak to her, but she said nothing. Gave nothing.

THEY LET me wander the ship as I pleased now. Apparently, I was no longer deemed a threat. Small wonder. Trapped inside a clumsy-featured slip of flesh as I was, what threat did I pose? I was only human. No more handcuffed walks for me. If crewmen were secretly monitoring, I didn't see them.

I went into the recreation room and helped crewmen hang white ribbon along the plaster walls. I did not speak. I had nothing valuable to contribute. Two females arranged plates, cloths, and metal utensils on ten round tables. Even spread out, the tabled area only occupied a quarter of the available space. It looked, as Isobel would put it, *silly*. A corpse of a ship, a hollowed-out husk, pretending to live.

When I wandered back to Isobel's room to talk, she wasn't

there. Her pristine bed had been made. Not a wrinkle marred the silk coverlet. Pillows cluttered the top in an 'ornamental' fashion. Three frosted champagne bottles lurked on her nightstand, sweating condensation. Cold. Fresh. Beside them, a gold corkscrew waited.

I knew it'd put Isobel in a bad mood, but I opened one of the bottles, carried it to her bathroom, and dumped it down the sink. Alcohol fumes filled the air.

Stupid.

Irrational.

Why did I care whether or not Dame Isobel drugged herself silly? My life would be easier if she were drunk.

I dumped the second bottle down the drain, heart fluttering, jaw tensed.

Illogical.

She could always order more. Me doing this made no difference. All I was doing was making my life harder. Stupid. Stupid, Fisherman.

I snatched up the third bottle—

My fingers brushed something on the backside of the bedstand. Smooth. Plastic. A raised disc with a protrusion.

I craned my head to see it.

Its glass eye glared. A small red light winked at me over the lens.

It was a small video camera.

The champagne bottle slipped out of my fingers. It hit the tile.

Crash!

Glass shards twinkled. Urine-colored alcohol fizzed, frothed, seethed out.

Isobel would never have a video camera in her room. Even with me there. Too risky. No reason for her to—she didn't care if I killed her. Someone else had placed this camera in a hidden location to videotape her in bed.

I felt sick.

What to do? Remove it? Tell Isobel? The video camera had captured me looking at it. The person knew I'd seen it, or would shortly.

I staggered out of Isobel's cabin. Down three floors, crewmen clattered around their quarters. Air purred through the vents. I made my way to the top room, the one with the window. Viewing room. Seeing Home would help me think.

Who wants a video camera in Isobel's room?

Someone had been watching us copulate.

I felt sicker. I shivered. Sweat stickied my skin. If I pressed a finger to my wrist, the skin wanted to cling. Beads of cold sweat dripped down my legs and torso.

Increment by increment, the ENS *Princess* slithered through white ice. Whining drills crushed the ice shelf ahead. Bits of ice bobbed in the black water. Jove blotted out half the sky, gases swirling in bands. Radiation nudged down from overhead. If I had my real eyes, I'd be seeing iridescent bands and waves—radiation skitters around corners as it pleases.

"You think you have a problem," Aeter said audibly.

I was alone, so I spoke aloud.

"Isobel's insane. I can't fix her. We're being monitored. Europa's humans are breeding bad ideas, and I can't solve their issues. What ever happened to Liore Hyung? Did you heal her?" I asked.

"Where is your skin, Little One?"

"In an inaccessible aquarium."

"Is it?"

Something sloshed by the drills below, loud enough to penetrate layers of metal.

From the slush of ocean and ice, a flesh-colored feeler emerged, half as thick as the ship. Brilliant pink villi furred the underside.

One of us. Another Fisherman was here, swimming right outside the ENS *Princess.*

I froze.

"Your agitated blood attracted notice, Little One," Aeter whispered. "When you sent it Home. Did you think I was the only one who would sense it?"

The feeler brushed along the side of the ship, caressing it. Villi writhed.

My skin. It's feeling for my skin.

But the crew would find the other Fisherman. They'd hurt them, the same way they'd hurt me, and—

I couldn't scream. Couldn't move.

"Stop them. They'll get imprisoned like me. Make them go away," I whispered.

"Now you don't want to be rescued?" Aeter said.

"But—

"You know they could destroy this piddling little hunk of metal."

The feeler lunged, smacking against the viewing room window. Window glass quivered. I stumbled. Flesh blanketed all. In the stark electric lighting, the villi looked drained, bloodless, deprived of life—samples of flesh smashed between glass.

Humans will capture you and keep us both in a lab for the rest of our existences.

I made my legs move over to the window and slammed my palm on it. Warmth saturated through the glass. Heat soaked into my skin.

(YOU!)

There was a brief *(YOU!) (good)* twinkle of recognition…from them. Not me. I probed. Who *was* this? Familiar, but unfamiliar. I stroked the glass, willing it to shatter. I'd never met this individual before, and had no memories of them…which wasn't possible. We all know each other, even if dimly.

I asked, *(Who are you?)*

They said, (*HELP YOU*)

They wanted to rip this ship to bits, curl around me, drag me under because I wasn't Home, that was the issue, something was wrong with me, but I needed (*HOME*) and then I'd look right—

"No, no, I don't have my skin," I murmured. "You'll end my existence if you do that. I can't change. I'm stuck as a human."

(*HUMAN*)

And a hot surge of rage stabbed through my forehead.

(*HUMAN!*)

"Why do you...what did they...why do you have this much emotion? You hate these humans?" I asked.

No other Fisherman currently hated humans as much as I currently did. I was fairly certain of that. Why was this one so angry? What experience did it have—

(*make it STOP*)

More pain through my right eye.

"They'll hurt you," I said. "Please go away. Hide."

The other Fisherman sent me a (*good*) warm caressing feeling, as if they were brushing my face. Then their feeler slithered down the viewing window, leaving no residue. It retreated back Home and into the slush.

Slush. Whining drills. Black sky. Jove.

Tears gushed down my cheeks.

Someone knows where I am. They'll tell others. There's hope. They came for me.

In. Out. I breathed, air pulling into and out of my lungs. In. Out. There was hope. It might even happen soon. Someone only needed to pry that aquarium apart before they destroyed the rest of the ship, so I access my skin...and then I'd be free.

Tell the other one. Aquarium first, I thought to Aeter.

"Done."

Yes. Yes, yes! I'd be free, and Isobel—

Oh, Isobel.

If I stayed, I could keep her alive. If I left, she'd die—either by killing herself, or being assassinated.

"You owe her nothing, Little One."

I know.

"Your judgement is clouded by hormones. I doubt you'll feel the same once you change form."

Fishermen care for each other, even when we change forms, I thought.

I started to feel guilt. I'd just told Aeter to command the other Fisherman to destroy this ship, killing everyone aboard. No. Not all of them deserved to die. The only one who'd wronged me was Isobel.

"Aeter," I thought, "Aeter, don't let them destroy the ship."

"Oh, *now* you say that?" Aeter said, "Hm. Hm."

"Have them wait close by. I'll tell the crew that it's a threat. They'll have to release my skin, and then I can leave without harming anyone."

With that, I went to find a crewman. I encountered Gavin as I stormed out of the viewing room.

"You!" I said.

He stopped, crossing his arms. "Yes?"

"There's a Fisherman in the water outside—"

"Did not see it."

"Of course you can't see it, it's underwater now—"

"The ship's sensors detect nothing."

"You don't understand. They can take a form the ship wouldn't be able to detect. They can mimic the form of anyone on board. If they decide to come in—"

"I don't see anything," Gavin said, each word deliberate, lacking emotion. "If I don't see anything, neither will anyone else. Do you understand?"

"Are you threatening me?"

He smiled at me, lips tight over his teeth. Overhead light cast shadows over his eyes and under his cheekbones. The silver hairs in his beard glinted amid the black. On the braided tails of it, yellow beads rocked back and forth from momentum. Besides us, the corridor lay empty.

He waited.

"…you want knowledge? That's what you're waiting for? You're bartering? You're a human. Humans don't do that," I said.

He waited. The smile did not change. Ship motors whined far below. He hadn't blinked for the last ten seconds.

"Humans barter knowledge, too, Fisherman. They do it less formally," he said.

"How did you become aware of knowledge barter?"

He smiled again, tilting his head.

"Argh!"

I threw my hands up. It accomplished nothing, but it felt good.

"Fine, Gavin. The skin in X-520 contains 34.5 million genetic memories, 2 million of which are unique forms. If you humans try to experiment with it, I'll rip you to shreds with these stupid little teeth—I will do it. I will manage it somehow," I snarled. "Three facts. There. Now tell me three."

"Two. Your last "fact" was an opinion. You won't hurt anyone. You're too passive. You've always been too passive, my friend. If you want to kill Dame Isobel, you have constant opportunities. You have not. You will not," he said sadly.

"You are not my friend," I said. "Do not call me that. It is inaccurate and insulting. My Friend would be ripping this ship apart to rescue me if they knew I was here."

Gavin sighed. He looked tired.

Why aren't you doing anything about the Fisherman outside the ship?" I asked.

He held up a finger. "Because there is no Fisherman outside the ship."

"You want to capture the other one, don't you? Hold them hostage, like me. Run experiments on us—"

He held up two fingers. "The Dame Family owns a multi-planetary skincare company."

No.

They'd begin capturing us. Now the humans knew to peel our skins.

I felt sick.

Even if Isobel set me free, they'd capture another Fisherman.

Oh. No. No.

Bolts of energy shot down my shoulders, into my fingers. My lips peeled back from my teeth. His throat bobbed. Looked chewable. Easy to crush. His fragile larynx. If I hit it hard enough—

I lunged towards him.

He sidestepped, grabbed my wrist, and threw me down. Pain, white-hot, surged through my knees. I struggled up. A syringe shone between his fingers. His hand gripped around my throat. Squeezed. Black dots exploded at the corners of my eyes. Hurt. I wheezed. I inhaled, got a needle-thin trickle of air.

Hot sting on my neck.

Lead-heavy blackness swelled up from the floor, dragged me down, down,

(down)

(!!!)

I WOKE in Isobel's cabin, in 'my' bed, in 'my' room, not hers. Had a pounding headache.

1:57 pm, said the electric clock on the bedside table.

Thick buzzing in my skull, I asked Aeter, "Was that a dream?"

"Everything is the Dream."

I amended my question.

"Was someone truly looking for me? Did another one of us find me?" I asked.

"You are also looking for yourself," Aeter said.

Had I seen a vision? Was the other Fisherman I'd interacted with an external reality, or a metaphor for my current state—trapped in a foreign body, reaching to find myself? My skin?

Riddles, paradoxes, half-truths, and symbols.

Frustrating.

I needed to find a crewman and ask. At least one of them would tell me whether or not another massive undersea entity had approached the ship, whether Gavin had lied to the captain or not. But Isobel. I was supposed to meet her at 2 pm.

Mouth sticky from sleep, I clambered out of bed. I walked down the little hallway to Isobel's room. Her door was shut. I knocked, heard no reply. The knob turned. I went in, closing the door behind me softly.

Celia and the white-uniformed Captain Anderson stood by Isobel's bed. Celia carried a hand-sized video player. Isobel wasn't here.

"What are you doing?" I asked.

I didn't know enough to be scared.

I hadn't put it together yet.

"We're here to take you to tea," Celia said, just as casual as always.

"What is 'tea'?"

"It's a snack time. It's downstairs."

"I'm supposed to meet Isobel here at two," I said.

"That's changed. You're meeting her downstairs for tea," Celia said.

"Humans. You're always changing details," I said.

She did not smile.

I went with them. Down to the bottom of the ENS *Princess*. X-520 lie nearby; my skin wanted me, I could feel it. Could sense me.

The room was small, composed of steel, and contained a single bed, toilet, and attached sink. A plastic tray and cup sat on the grime-encrusted floor.

"Where are the tea foods?" I asked. "Where's Isobel?"

"Coming. Wait for them," Celia said.

I didn't realize where'd they taken me until they closed and bolted the metal door behind me. I turned and read the inscription spray-painted on the far wall.

Brig.

CHAPTER 6

I slept. I dreamed:

The humans are intruders.

True, true, very true, Aeter says softly, *Do you remember?*

I remember life before them.

No, before that, and soft as mucous something brushes inside my skin—the foreign one; I am skinless.

I remember: scuttling across ice, pressure at my back, a vague wash of sunlight, the taste of radiation—*burnt ozone,* my human brain whispers—

Heaving my small limp body forward. The sticky exterior layer of me glues itself to the ice as I ambulate. I tear myself free, continue on. A black fissure in the ice. Slithering into it;

Do you remember?

Impact.

Rush of warmth.

(good)

Tingling all over.

(good) *(Home)* working through me, soothing, warmth, insu-lation, suddenly it was easy to move, I could think and then I moved in a direction, limbs *(I have limbs)* working, pressure

increasing as I went deeper, sprouting gills, bands of electro-magnetism popping into existence as I grew eyes to perceive them.

Do you remember growing your skin? Aeter asks.

I grew it?

None of you ever remember, Aeter chides, *I thought you had better neural tissue than that. Naughty Little Ones.*

I grew it.

I always gave you the capacity to grow your skin.

I grew it?

Aeter doesn't reply. Aeter doesn't need to.

IN THAT BRIG, I got two, maybe three hours, of dreaming, where every position ached, and heat festered in me. I shivered. Sweat soaked my thin dress.

I grew my skin. I have the capacity to generate another skin.

My fingers trembled around the edge of the wool bed blanket.

Then came a knock at the door.

I sat up. The steel door clanked open. A meaty crewman with tied-back hair clomped into the brig, flanked by two others. He carried a blank video screen. They shut the door.

"Dame Isobel would like to speak to you," he rasped.

"She can come here," I said.

"For her safety, she will communicate through the video screen."

"Safety? We've been sleeping together for the last two weeks."

Then I remembered I wasn't supposed to say that.

"In a shared bed. Only sleep occurred in the shared bed. The guest bed was broken. We had to share a bed, so that is why it happened," I said.

"You murdered Gavin LaBeouf."

Murdered?

"No. I didn't," I said.

"Dame Isobel will be with you shortly—

"I didn't kill Gavin."

"They found his body in the viewing room. His tools and clothing were found in Dame Isobel's quarters."

"Including his e-key?" I asked.

Meaty glanced at the other crewmen. One of them pursed his lips into a white line.

Dame Isobel's face filled the video screen. Blood vessels contaminated the whites of her eyes, making her blue irises blaze. Cosmetic clumped her eyelashes.

"You could've told me no," she said, sniffling.

I squinted at her.

"You didn't have to kill him for that e-key. I still would've gotten it for you. Even if you said no—"

"Isobel, I didn't kill him."

"He unspooled his intestines by himself?"

"What?"

"You know what you did. Why did you do this before—"

Her lips trembled. She scrubbed her palm over them.

She said, "I have that interview in fifteen minutes. I can't do this now. I'll talk to you in a few—"

"There's a video camera hidden behind your bedside table. I saw Celia and the captain talking by your bed, and then they took me here. And there's another Fisherman here. They're outside the ship," I said. "They may have boarded, assumed someone else's form, and murdered Gavin for the e-key in an attempt to free me."

"The crew didn't report encountering any other Fishermen," she said, tone clipped and cold.

"Do you trust them?" I asked.

"They wouldn't lie."

"Why not?"

She shook her head. "I have the interview. I need to go."

"I hope you think about Liore Hyung before you speak."

"She's missing."

"Missing?" I asked. "As in *dead?*"

"Liore disappeared. She's been missing for the last three days. Found out from her family when I called a few hours ago. I call her every week. She doesn't speak much. Thinks we were childhood friends, and that's why she can't remember me well. Now she's missing. Probably dead. They found blobs of meat goo in her bed, between the sheets. Like snail slime. She just... laid down to sleep, and then she..."

"Isobel—"

"Aeter cured her. She's not suffering anymore," Isobel whispered.

The video screen went black.

Then, the crewmen left my cell, taking everything with them.

I ASKED Aeter if They'd liquified Liore Hyung. No response. Shortly after, another trio of crewmen entered, and left a plastic tray of food and a bottle of freshwater.

Shivering, muscles twitching, I asked, "Was there another Fisherman in the water?"

"No," one of them said.

"There are cameras in the viewing room. Check the footage I saw someone—"

"While you were pulling Gavin's intestines out of his belly?"

I sat up. "Does it make logical sense for me to do something like that?"

A crewman shifted his weight, hand on the door.

"If my goal was to obtain Gavin's e-key to free my skin, and therefore leave this ship, why would I waste precious time disemboweling him? I'd slit his throat and be done. Or smash his skull on a metal ledge," I said.

"How the hell should I know what you like doing?"

Someone had murdered Gavin, and I had a fairly good idea who. The other Fisherman, who hated humans. The other Fisherman could've easily changed form, slithered up a wastewater pipe, and out of a sink tap. Any number of ways it could've been done. Once aboard the ship, they'd gone to find me in the viewing room, encountered Gavin, and brutally killed him.

There was a currently a shapeshifting, human-despising entity aboard this ship. And it wasn't me. What if they hurt Isobel?

I felt nauseous and clammy.

"There's another Fisherman on board this ship. For the safety of everyone here, I suggest you find them before they cause a massacre," I said.

He slammed the door shut. The cell door vibrated softly from the force. I scrambled out of bed to the food tray. Scrambled eggs steamed in a paper boat. Vegetables cooked and slathered in sugar syrup filled the other half of the boat. My mouth watered, but my stomach hurt. I wanted to vomit. I ignored the food.

Another knock on the door.

I watched Captain Anderson and wrinkled Celia enter.

"So many visitors," I said. "But you're all visitors to me. You can't exist here without metal, supplied atmospheres, lead shielding, and a hair-thin temperature range..."

"There was an electromagnetic pulse that destroyed most of our video cameras," Captain Anderson said.

He had a clear, low-pitched voice. He stood erect, shoulders back, like a non-living chunk of ice. Black, cropped facial hair darkened the lower half of his face and neck. He was bald. The top of his skull gleamed as if polished. Eyebrows thick as my thumb loomed over his deep-set eyes. His jumpsuit looked similar to the crew's, except for it being white.

"Of course there was. Nobody saw Gavin being killed," I said slowly. "I want you to listen to me very carefully. I contacted the god who created Fishermen, and They responded. They sent others to free me. Many of our forms feed on energy. It is simple for us to generate an electromagnetic pulse. I didn't kill Gavin. If I did, I certainly wouldn't be inefficient and pull out his intestines. So. There is another Fisherman aboard this ship, one with a functional skin. They can shape-shift into any form. They can look like anyone. You cannot injure or kill them."

Celia paled. Captain Anderson folded his arms.

"You have two options. Return my skin and let me go, or wait for the dead bodies to start appearing," I said.

"The e-key to X-520 is missing," he said.

"Find it."

"We've been searching the ship for the last five hours."

"You acknowledge that I didn't murder Gavin. Why am I still here? Why did you lock me in here?"

"You killed Gavin," Celia said.

"No. I didn't. The other Fisherman did," I said.

"Show the video footage," Captain Anderson said.

Celia produced a pocket-sized video screen and turned it on.

"You said the cameras were destroyed by an electromagnetic pulse," I said.

Grainy video footage appeared tinted blue. Me standing in the viewing room, facing the window, thin white gown fluttering in the air vent's breeze. Back facing the camera, pale hair rippling. Footsteps echoed. Gavin appeared in the bottom left corner of the frame.

Static exploded over the screen.

Then the viewing room again. I was no longer in sight. There was only Gavin. Gavin, flat on his back, spasming. Worm-like coils spooled on the floor around him. Blood puddled, blooming across the floor, black in the tinted video footage.

"We found you in the viewing room shortly after the time-stamp on that footage. Gavin's body had been moved to a storage closet. Traces of your saliva were on the floor. You licked his blood up, then went back to your room. We lied to get you to come quietly, until we could figure out what happened," Anderson said.

"There is no 'we', and I don't appreciate your forced usage of the word. This footage is obviously fraudulent. It cuts off at a convenient time. You cannot see my face at any point," I said. "I wonder, Captain—who hid the video camera in Dame Isobel's room?"

I looked at Celia. "It had to be someone that Isobel trusted."

She smiled in an (*unpleasant*) way, sweat acrid smelling. Blink, blink, blink, went her eyes. Too quick. I could practically taste the cortisol oozing off her.

"Isobel's parents wanted to see what she would do if they gave her a little freedom," Celia said.

"It was you. You spied on us during sex," I said.

Her nose wrinkled. "Isobel knows what she's allowed and not allowed to do."

"She thought you were her friend."

"No friends among the Dame family."

A sick feeling sprouted in my stomach. It closed my throat up.

"You filmed us. Having sex," I said.

"Nothing personal."

"Isobel could be lobotomized like Liore, or hanged. You're aware of that. It *is personal, Celia.*"

Anderson twitched. He hid his facial expression after a millisecond, but I caught it: contorted face, disgust. At Isobel and I, or Celia?

"Why did you really put me here? Was it so Isobel and I would be separated?"

"Did you murder Gavin for the e-key, Fisherman?" Anderson said.

"It doesn't make sense for me to have murdered him," I said.

"We'll agree to disagree—"

"Where's the body now?"

"In the ship's morgue."

I bared my teeth. "Are you absolutely sure? Do you have anyone monitoring that body?"

"Why would we?"

"You *idiots.* That's the other Fisherman. They hid in the storage closet and mimicked Gavin's cadaver."

"Then where did Gavin's actual cadaver go?" Celia asked.

I sighed. "The other Fisherman probably ate it."

Anderson muttered, "There wasn't another Fisherman..."

"You're thinking out loud. I can hear it. You sound unsure. There was something, wasn't there? The sensors picked something up. You had an intuition," I said.

"The Portside crew heard brief sounds outside of the ship, as well as minor impacts. But Gavin investigated and said there wasn't anything abnormal. Engine issues. Ice..."

"They could've slithered into the ship's bilge, gone up a pipe, and entered. Easily."

"Or...into the wastewater drains," Anderson whispered.

"Precisely. Consider a few more questions. If I did kill Gavin, then where did all the blood on the floor go? From when Gavin was gutted? How did I rip his peritoneal cavity apart without a sharp blade? I have no effective teeth or claws. Tell me. How did I do it? You didn't report any blood when you 'sedated' me. Why wasn't I covered in blood? In fact, why should I believe that either of you didn't frame me for the murder? Was Gavin getting sympathetic to my cause? Did you think he'd hand over the e-key, give me my skin, and release me? Was that an unallowable occurrence, because of the chance that I'd ruin the Dame family's reputation, should I escape?" I said.

Celia shook. Her throat worked.

I smiled, and it felt *unpleasant.* "Don't worry. I'm a *disgusting alien,* despite the fact that I was created here, and you humans weren't. Who would ever believe anything I have to say?"

"Fisherman. Tell me. Did you murder Gavin LaBeouf?" Anderson asked.

"You know I didn't. The most logical explanation is what I explained, and you know it. There's another Fisherman on board. Let me out of here, and I'll talk to them. I'll get my skin. We'll leave without any more violence. I'm sorry they killed Gavin," I said.

Captain Anderson stared at me for a long, long moment. Then he unlocked the brig door.

He motioned into the hallway. "Morgue's upstairs, fourth level, below the crew quarters. Go. I'll isolate the crew in the lunchroom. Won't bother you. I need to contact LaBeouf's family."

"What if we need to communicate?" I said.

He tore a handheld radio from his belt. "Take it. Press and hold the red button to talk. Channel 3. Keep it there."

A shrill scream came from upstairs.

Isobel!

My stomach wrenched.

"Isobel," I said.

Celia nudged me out. I let her.

"I'll find Isobel," she said. "Go!"

I bolted towards the stairwell.

Oh, Isobel.

No time.

My palm slapped the stairwell handle. Yanked it open, ran upstairs. *Clank-clank-clank.* Breathing hurt. Heat built in my calves. I bumped into two crewmen as I went around the corner, shoved past them, up, up, throat going dry, shivering, head pulsing like a fist in my brain, squeezing, releasing.

The orange-painted handrail chilled my hand; as my palm glided along the rail, it clung. I had sticky, gluey, tacky human skin.

pulse-pulse-pulse

Up a floor. I burst through the door.

Nobody existed in the corridor. Rust-colored lights trickled thinly overhead. At the end, a doorway blazed with white, fluorescent light. Unreal. It looked like *(paper)*

Arrangements, read the paint above the doorway.

I plunged in.

White room. White floors and walls, floor drain at the center. Stink of bleach. Steel drawers rowed the far wall.

One of the drawers gaped open.

Blood streaked the platform that had held Gavin's cadaver. Smears of blood trailed to the door.

Gavin's body was gone.

To be certain, I opened the other drawers. Nothing lurked in any of them. They stank of alcohol, bleach, and under that, metal.

Blood.

The other Fisherman had left the morgue.

I pressed the handheld button and snapped, "Body's gone."

Mechanical crackling.

"You're sure? Did you open the other drawers?" Anderson said.

"Yes."

I squeezed and released the handheld rhythmically, thinking. As I let go, strings of iridescent slime stretched from my skin to the plastic.

I still feel feverish.

If my dream held truth, then I was…growing another skin.

"What does the other Fisherman want?" Anderson asked.

His voice softened, slurred. "I read the stories. When I was a kid. The ones they tell you in school. Fisherman, turning into mermaids, luring people to their deaths—"

"Untrue. Those ships antagonized *us* first. We dragged them down under the water, plucked the humans out with our tentacles, and ate them whole. It only happened three times ever. They fired missiles at us, Anderson," I said.

"—granting wishes, you know some guy with Stage IV pancreatic cancer saw one out a cruise liner window and waved it at it. Said it waved back. Said next check-up, his cancer was *gone*, fucking *gone*."

"I don't have time for this," I said.

"Is—is it true? Did—"

"Aeter. Not us. Aeter does what Aeter wants, and Aeter sees through our eyes. Sometimes Aeter heals because it amuses Them."

Harsh breathing. A chuckle.

"If you get a chance, ask Aeter to fix an eight-year-old kid named Saul Anderson. Leukemia. Please."

"Aeter has already heard."

"Just fuckin' ask, too."

"Gather the crewmen into the lunchroom and instruct them to remain inside. I need to find the other Fisherman," I said, then released the button.

Get Isobel to safety. Find her.

"Did you hear that, Aeter?" I said.

Silence.

I turned and sprinted upstairs, where Isobel had screamed. If nothing else, I had to find her. It was illogical. I knew it. Stupid. Wasting time. The true priority was to find the other Fisherman, and I didn't even know what I'd do with Isobel when I found her, besides escort her to the lunchroom with the crew.

I kept a brisk pace down the hallway through the crew quarters. Nobody accosted me. Besides my footsteps and ragged breathing, no sound existed. Isobel had stopped screaming.

I assessed the facts.

Fact: There was another Fisherman. Gavin's cadaver had revived and ventured out of the morgue, leaving a trail of blood. The other Fisherman had not warmly greeted me from Home. They'd been watching me suffer here. For weeks. Landlocked in a foreign skin.

What a stupid thought.

What would another Fisherman do to harm me?

Fact: Aeter, my parent and creator-god, let all of this happen. I knew the *how*, but not the *why*.

Ten minutes had elapsed since speaking with Anderson.

Another scream shrilled ahead. Isobel. It came from her quarters.

I eased the blue-painted door open and entered, as if slithering through a crack.

"Isobel?" I said.

Sobbing. Snuffling, wet breathing sounds in her room. I padded through the little hallway. Her door lay open. In the unlit room, two female silhouettes sat on the bed. Isobel. Celia. Isobel wept, comforted by Celia. In her lap sat Gavin's e-key.

"We have to go to the lunchroom with the crewmen," Celia soothed. "It doesn't matter now."

"I'm waiting for her," Isobel said.

"It is a creature. Not a she. It doesn't care about you any more than a shark does. It's like a wild animal. Come along."

"Not until I give her the e-key. She deserves to be free."

"Paloma's tumors choked him from the inside out within a week," Celia said.

"That wasn't her fault."

"Isobel, these creatures are alien and dangerous."

She laughed. "So dangerous. Paloma's dead. Liore's dead. But who cut Gavin open? We both know it wasn't the Fisherman, Celia."

Isobel?

I flicked the light on.

Isobel startled. Celia remained steady. One hand nestled in her lap. Another hand gripped Isobel's jeweled, gauze-covered shoulder.

Barely visible among her hair follicles, sprays of dried blood speckled her lower legs.

I could smell it.

"Isobel?" I asked.

"You. Oh, you. I got you the e-key," she said.

"Why is there blood on your legs?"

Her glazed eyes looked like flat steel disks. "I thought I got it all."

"There's another Fisherman on board. They are hostile. You need to go to the lunchroom with the crew members."

I'd mention Celia's betrayal before I left.

"Another Fisherman? Oh. That explains a few silly things I noticed," Isobel said.

I guided her to the door. She let me, limp as a mannequin. Celia slid something metallic into her pocket as stood and followed us.

"Noticed?" I asked.

"When I killed Gavin," she said dreamily. "I love you."

CHAPTER 7

"*Y*ou did what?" I asked.

She said she loves me.

Bubbly excitement tingled in my chest.

She killed Gavin, but she said she loves me.

Why, oh why, was I this sentimental? Right now? When Isobel had confessed to murdering Gavin?

Inside me, thoughts sang, *she loves me! She loves me!*

How stupid. How human. She'd captured me, imprisoned me, ripped off a part of my anatomy, acted erratically, but because she formed a string of three meaningless sounds together, I suddenly felt happy?

Stupid glands, squirting out stupid neurotransmitters for a stupid, singular brain.

"You killed Gavin?" I asked.

My palm was malformed after clutching Isobel's arm. Skin shifted like sticky putty.

I thought, *(eyes)*

But no eyes bubbled from my skin. I tried again, thought *(eyes, teeth)*. A tingling ran down my torso and scalp, but nothing happened. Nothing formed.

"I tried to ask Gavin for his e-key, but he wouldn't give it to me. I knew he probably wouldn't," Isobel said.

"The video footage—"

"I control Anderson and Celia. I told them to sedate you and take you to the brig, and then—"

"You slit Gavin's belly open? And then pulled out his intestines?"

"I'm sorry I had to put you in the brig. I only needed a few hours."

I stopped. Iridescence gleamed over my skin. That was abnormal. It resembled my true skin now…

"That seems strange for you," I heard myself say.

A flicker of something warmed back of my throat. A taste of salt

(*home*)

Bone.

Spike.

Something hard sprouted from my forearm. Slicked in blood, a spur of human bone emerged. The tip prickled. Grooves lined the fresh bone.

A smile spread over my face. I felt it.

Do it again.

"Fisherman?" Isobel asked.

Another bone spike shot out from my forearm, where the wrist melded into the palm.

schlorp.

It nudged tendons as it slid out. I thought (*back*) and it retreated under the skin again.

In. Out.

Snick.

Snick.

I'd grown a new skin, but why wasn't it doing what I wanted it to? All it could form was (*human*) but in different permutations. Why? Where had the memories of my other forms gone?

It's a new skin. It doesn't have any.

You must understand. This never happened to any of us before—and we would know, we barter knowledge. Never had anyone considered the possibility of losing their skin, let alone *growing a new one.*

I am logical. I am not what humans call "creative". I think in interlocking chains of sensory-based facts. Why diverge from fact? Dreams are slanted facts, not looping impossibility. *What if? Why?* Are not thoughts I typically have.

But the truth was in front of me: I had grown a new skin.

My heart quickened. It pounded through my lips.

Could I go home?

I dreamed, *(form)*. Nothing happened. Nothing came. Nothing shifted. I visualized my summer form, eyes and mass and tentacles.

Nothing. My form didn't change.

This skin didn't have the genetic memory of my old one. I trailed a finger down my skin. I tasted sweat. Tasted *(human)*.

It was a nascent hide, still ripening. I probed internally, found only *(human)* and *(silkworm)*. Neither of those could breathe underwater or exist without oxygen. I still had to absorb the memories from my old skin, which was locked in that vile aquarium. Even after *growing a new skin,* I still couldn't go Home.

A guttural scream formed deep in my esophagus.

HOME! I WANT TO GO HOME!

I swallowed the scream back. I had so many screams inside me but none of them could be expressed. So many screams.

"Isobel, what about the video footage?" I asked.

"The computer programs generated fake footage for me. I used a rough of my body, because it's been saved in the files. For the faked LUV footage, I didn't have your face, though, so I stuck to back shots."

I had grown a new skin. Isobel had murdered a man to help

me. She said she *loved me,* and for the first time, those words seemed authentic.

"Did you do the interview with LUV?" I asked, which was stupid.

It didn't matter whether she had or not, but it felt like it did.

"No," she said, standing. "I canceled it."

"Good."

"No, not good," Celia snapped.

"Celia filmed us having intercourse, Isobel."

Isobel blinked. "What?"

Celia circled Isobel's waist with her arm. She pulled her close, as if comforting a child. Her face pressed into Isobel's fine, pearl-pale hair. Isobel let her.

Something metal glinted between Celia's fingers.

Her hand flitted to Isobel's throat.

I didn't realize she'd slit Isobel's throat until it was too late.

A red line appeared there, thin as silk thread. It stretched from ear to ear, a red thread choker necklace.

Necklace?

Red bubbles formed along the line. Isobel blinked again. She patted her throat. Blood smeared her fingers. Blood bubbles popped, getting on her silver-painted nails.

No.

No, no, this is a dream.

The dribble grew to a gush. Blood curtained from her slit throat. Isobel's knees buckled. Celia lowered her to the ground.

Blood rivulet between her breasts, soaking her dress—

NO!

A strangled gargling came out of me. I couldn't move.

Celia.

Celia was waiting to assassinate Isobel.

Dame Serena's threat to Isobel had been real. Celia had been given orders to assassinate Isobel for the reputation of the Dame family if Isobel didn't comply with Serena's threat. That video footage. It'd been captured to finalize the agreement. Isobel had one last chance to behave, according to Dame Serena. Isobel had been videotaped not behaving. Isobel had canceled her interview with LUV. Oh, Isobel. Isobel!

Snick.

Snick.

Bone spikes extended, retracted, extended, to the beating of my heart.

Snick.

Snick.

The e-key lay next to Isobel's knee. Celia grabbed it. She still kneeled, holding Isobel as she bled out. Celia held the e-key up to me.

I took it. Hot blood daubed my hands.

Celia gestured to Isobel's face. "Take her eye. Get past the retinal locks."

I did not move.

"Go. I know you'll never ruin the Dame family's reputation. Take your skin, and leave," she said.

"No."

"That's all you want, Fisherman. Now, go—"

"No!"

My yell filled the corridor.

Isobel's bleeding had stopped. Her eyelids fluttered. More red bubbles appeared at her throat.

How much blood do humans have? I can put it back in her. I can fix her. I can heal her. Isobel.

Snick.

Snick.

Both spikes shot out, reaching to my fingertips.

Isobel, dead.

(farther)

Bone calcified inside my shoulder joints. Segments formed, ready to click together.

Snick.

Snick.

They extended an arm's length out. Retreated. Clicked back into place.

Celia opened her mouth to speak again.

Isobel.

My arm twitched up. The spike shot out and plunged between Celia's lips. It emerged from the base of her skull, slicked in blood and spinal fluid, beaded in clumps of whitish brainstem. Her teeth clamped around the spike. They scraped as her jaw spasmed.

Snick.

I aimed for her right eye. I skewered my other spike through it, tasting *(salty) (fatty)* as it slithered from eye to brain, crunching past skull. Hair parted around the spike. Red smeared on silver. In. Out.

Urine darkened her pants. She slumped. The weight of her settled onto my spikes. I retracted them. Celia collapsed onto the floor like so much raw, limp meat.

"Isobel," I said hoarsely.

In my chest it ached. It should not ache. There was no reason for it to hurt, no damage, but it did.

Isobel had no pulse. I hovered over her fine lips, but she did not breathe. That pearl-white hair haloed her head within the puddle of blood. Already she looked like a mural, or a legend, to be painted on a wall, reminders of a dead era.

Isobel.

I picked up the e-key, and I left her there, because I couldn't do anything more adequate. I wouldn't mutilate her body by removing an eye. With my new skin, I could mimic her eyes perfectly.

Isobel, Isobel.

Going down the steps, to X-520, e-key almost slipping out of my fingers, I shivered. I couldn't cry yet. That would come later.

At least she wasn't suffering anymore, but what kind of thin comfort was that? She shouldn't have suffered the way she had. Now she was dead. I hadn't stopped Celia in time.

Stupid me.

Inefficient.

Inadequate. I had failed.

Tears burned my eyes. I wiped them away. No time. Get my old skin from the aquarium. Absorb its data. Find the other Fisherman on board. *Why,* I would ask, *Why do this? What purpose did any of this serve?*

I'd hold these wretched humans accountable.

Then, and only then, would I return home.

I pressed the red button on the handheld. "Captain Anderson?"

Crackling noises.

"Fisherman, did you plan this?" Anderson said.

"Plan what?"

A note of anger thickened his tone. "Gavin's not on this ship. Gavin was never on this ship. When I called his family to tell them he'd died, they asked me what the fuck I was talking about. He's been dead since the solstice. Blew his brains out two months ago."

I dropped the handheld. It hit the floor. Shaking, I picked it up.

"Are you certain?" I asked.

"They voxxed over the autopsy pictures. What do you want? I'll give you anything."

"My skin—"

"You planned this the entire time. You planted the other Fisherman among the crew before we launched—it was so sudden, we didn't check credentials like usual. Then, you let yourself get captured, knowing that you had an ally aboard," he said.

"I'm as shocked as you," I said.

"What do you want? Money? Power? Humans off Europa? You were planning on taking Dame Isobel hostage, weren't you?"

"Those are all logical plans, but I had no part in any of it."

Silence, except for his breathing.

"You don't have your skin. Right now, you heal at a standard human rate. If I shoot you, you'll die," he said. "Remember that. I'll give you one hour to leave this ship. Stay out of the lunchroom. After that, if you're still on board, we start hunting."

Click.

I considered everything. A new framework of logic and fact needed to be formed.

New information: "Gavin LaBeouf" was not the true Gavin LaBeouf. There had never been a Gavin LaBeouf aboard this ship. Another Fisherman had mimicked his form the entire time.

It made sense. Possibly, Anderson could be lying, but it would serve no purpose. Unless Anderson was also a Fisherman. Unless—no, stick to the facts.

It also explained where "Gavin's" cadaver had gone—the other Fisherman had simply allowed Isobel to "kill" them, kept themselves alive, healed, and left the morgue.

The encounter with the Fisherman in the water had been a dream. That was the best explanation. Without my skin, I couldn't perceive another Fisherman unless they wanted me to, but on a primal level, I must've realized that "Gavin" was a Fisherman. Or perhaps I was crazy. Something rotting or warping inside my single brain. One brain. How stupid. No wonder humans struggled.

I discarded that particular theory: I am not human; I am not crazy. Aeter could send dreams. That was more likely. But why?

Too many holes in my logic.

Factual errors. Where?

Why had everyone let me suffer for *weeks?*

I descended to X-520 and the stench of rubbing alcohol (*bad*) drove spikes up my nostrils.

X-520 loomed. Nearby, the brig door hung ajar. Trails of puddled water crisscrossed the blue-painted steel floor, gleaming.

I crouched, touched one, and

(*mitozoa*)

(*life*)

(*HOME*)

I flinched back, fingers dripping.

This water hadn't come from the ship's sterile reserves. It writhed with microscopic organisms. Not Earth ones. Native microorganisms. Delicious little creatures twitched within, bound by a curve of surface tension; generations of life contained within glass.

It was Home.

This water had come from the oceans outside. Something had carried it in—dribbled it in.

Clanging sounds twanged out of the brig, echoing.

Twang! Twang!

It sounded like bone hitting metal. Not metal hitting metal.

"You knew," a female voice said tonelessly.

The flat female voice said it again, from inside the brig. It sounded...familiar? But from where? I didn't know any other humans. Who was this?

"You knew."

More blows. Rhythmic, twang-twang-SnAP!

The dry snap of human bone breaking.

A hissing exhale. Gob of saliva smacking into steel. She'd spat on the ground.

She seethed, "You knew, *Isobel*."

I entered the brig, and the female twisted to face me, snarling.

She was nude. She had clear dark eyes. Black, straight hair

curtained her face. Her fatless body was stringed with quivering muscle.

My stomach dropped.

It's HER!

No. No, this can't be—

"Liore," I said, "Liore Hyung."

CHAPTER 8

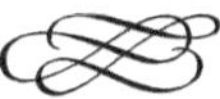

 *H*er eyes widened; for a second, she thought I was Isobel, I could see it. Then she tilted her head, blinking.

(*hello*)

Warmth slithered up my back, tingling.

(*YOU*)

That same feeling from before, as perceived through the viewing room window. Affection. Recognition.

Liore smiled at me, (*YOU*)

The Fisherman from the water.

"Give me your hand," I snapped.

Still smiling, she did. Something hard poked my palm. A tooth. It protruded from a nodule of gum tissue at the base of her pinky.

Iridescence glistened over her skin.

The genetic memories tickled.

(*human*)

(*summer-early-water—*)

That was it. I copied Liore's clumsy (*summer-early-water*) form and integrated it into my skin. Now it understood the framework of skin and flesh villi, the silicon-base of the form. She had no other memories encoded within her skin. Such a novelty. Every other Fisherman had millions. Tens of millions.

If the real Liore Hyung had been replaced by a Fisherman, like Gavin, "she" would have millions of stored forms. Not two. Unless she had her skin stolen and been forced to grow a new one, too. Yes. Which would also account for her abnormal hatred of humans. It made sense…

And yet…I did not know this Fisherman.

All Fishermen know each other or know of each other. Aeter hadn't created new Fishermen in eons. When we reproduced—a rare occurrence—we created offspring of our current form, not other Fishermen. Our offspring lacked skin and therefore could not change. Only Aeter bestowed skin.

"I saw you earlier. In the water," I said.

She stroked my arm, savoring the skin. Her pupils dilated.

"Pretty," she crooned. "I can taste it."

"Was that you?"

"Why were you miserable? Why didn't you break the window? You could've gone home," she said.

My pulse jittered. "You're the other Fisherman? You pretended to be Gavin?"

"Gavin?"

"Are you Liore Hyung?" I asked.

You're asking for information like a human, and she isn't barter-ing. A Fisherman would barter with me.

Aeter, what is going here?

"Yeah. Liore Hyung. That was me…" she said, gaze unfo-cused. "Before I went down the drain."

Humans used a lot of colorful figurative language. This was not one of those times, and the individual in front of me was not human.

"Down the drain?" I asked.

"Because I couldn't figure out how to break the window and

get into the water outside. They had people babysitting me. I had to go home. The bed was full of slime. So, I told the minder that I had to pee, I'd wet the bed. I was doing that a lot after they fucked up my brain. They said okay, they'd get new sheets, and left. I went to the bathtub and slipped down the drain. Aeter told me the wastewater goes to home," Liore said.

"You couldn't have pretended to be Gavin LaBeouf, because 'he' was on the ship before you were reported missing. You didn't take on Gavin's form..." I said, musing aloud.

"Who's Gavin?" Liore asked.

"You were born human?"

"Yes."

At the base of her collarbone lay a small, folded indent. It bloomed open, folds parting and a single human eye blinked at me. The black iris and shape were analogous to the eyes in her sockets.

Near the ceiling, the brig's clock said *11:15.*

30 minutes left.

I rubbed my thumb over her extra eye. "A mistake."

"I forgot how to put everything together how it was before," she said.

"It is adequate. For now. You will learn."

"Aeter started whispering to me in my sleep. A few weeks ago. I had...these dreams. Felt sick. Then I went down the drain. I don't know how it happened. I was just happy I could think again."

A few weeks ago? Didn't Isobel wish for Liore to be healed a few days ago?

"You went Home, and then what?" I asked.

"I shifted. I said I wanted to find Isobel. Aeter guided me here. Where's Isobel?"

Dead.

I couldn't tell her. I needed Liore docile while I worked everything out. I did not need emotional outbursts, inefficiency, or agitated crewmen gunning this poor Little One down. Evidently, Liore had been the Fisherman greeting me from the water. That hadn't been a dream. Which did not solve the mystery of Gavin the Fisherman. Isobel had apparently "murdered" Gavin and framed me for it. "Gavin" had pretended to die, healed in the morgue, and simply walked out when the opportunity came. So. There was a conspiracy here. To what end? Liore seemed too naïve, too fresh, to have a willing role in it. One fact was clear: Aeter had granted Isobel's wish and healed Liore—in the most efficient way possible to Aeter. Convert the human, then heal the new Little One.

In Their half-conscious, half-dreaming state, Aeter had not created any new Fishermen in the last one-hundred-thousand years. Earth years, listener. I did the math for you. For your edification, I myself have lived around a hundred and fifty thousand years.

Current priorities, in order: Get Liore off this ship, hunt down "Gavin", root out an explanation, and…Isobel…

How would I hold anyone accountable for Isobel's death? For her life? Would I go ashore, slither into Dame Serena's water supply, into her drinking glass, down her gullet? Rip her apart from the inside out? That wouldn't solve anything long term.

Liore Hyung was safe and healthy. I could ensure she stayed that way, for Isobel's sake.

Oh, Isobel.

Liore embraced me, nuzzling her head into the divot between my collarbones. Her lovely skin prickled against mine.

"Where'd the others go?" Liore said.

"Migrating. Come with me."

"Not 'til I find Isobel."

I lied, "I don't know where Isobel went. Let me get my old skin, and then I'll take you back home."

"No."

"You misunderstand. I wasn't asking," I said.

She pulled away. "Make me—"

The radio crackled. I lifted it and pressed the button.

"Anderson?" I asked.

Screams came from the speaker.

Multiple screams at once.

Wet, fleshy smacking.

Gurgling.

A soft *rat-tat-tat* sound. Gunfire cracked. Once. Twice.

Liore hissed. I gripped the radio, knuckles blanching.

"Fisherman," Anderson said, above the shrieks, the *schlorp-schlorp* of tearing flesh. His breathing bubbled. "I won't be hunting you down after all."

"Anderson, I had nothing to do with—"

"I started streaming the video camera footage in the lunch-room after I rounded up the crew. It's live all over Europa right now. Everyone's seeing this. They're gonna exterminate every last one of you alien motherfuckers—"

Coughing. "—every last one of you, including the Dame Family—"

The radio crackled off.

Liore had been the Fisherman in the water. Didn't mean there wasn't another one aboard.

Liore and I glanced at each other.

Then we sprinted for the stairs.

ISOBEL'S BODY WAS GONE.

My face contorted for a split second. I masked it.

We had passed by Celia's cadaver, both of us panting, and Liore stopped. She sweated blood. It jeweled her skin like rubies.

"I'm hungry," she said.

"We need to hurry."

"Won't save them. They're already dead. Fuck 'em. Fuck 'em all," she said.

Where did Isobel's body go?

I felt sick.

Liore crouched next to Celia's corpse. Beads of blood dotted her forehead and upper lip. I didn't criticize her for it. Blood could also work via evaporative cooling like sweat. Poor little Liore had never constructed sweat glands before; who was I to insult her first attempt?

"I never trusted her. Always hung around Isobel and I, even if Isobel asked her to go do something else," Liore said.

"We need to hurry."

She shrugged. Her torso split open from mons pubis to sternum. Organs glistened red within. Flesh-colored tentacles exploded from the cavity and plunged into Celia's ruined eye socket. Two coiled around neck and head, supporting it.

"I'm hungry," Liore said, innocent as a newborn.

I had no rebuttal.

She feasted. It took her ten seconds to reduce the top half of Celia's cadaver to stripped bone. She slurped brain from skull. Eye from socket.

Where's Isobel's body?

No drag marks or blood dirtied the floor. It looked like Isobel had never died. Similar to "Gavin". Had Isobel actually died, or had "Gavin" been mimicking her?

Or had "Gavin" simply consumed Isobel's corpse?

We are not sentimental about that.

My teeth ground.

"Gavin", my friend. Whoever you turn out to be. I hope you weren't stupid enough to mimic Isobel and pretend to die in front of me.

Aeter rumbled audibly in my ear, "They could have kept you

in a lab and peeled off your new skins as you grew them. Forever."

"What is going on, Aeter?" I asked.

"Do you like the human society on Europa?"

"It causes damage to its members."

"Mmmm."

"It is an organism in and of itself," I said.

"An efficient organism," Aeter said.

And the answer finally came to me—the question I had asked Dame Serena. Why? Why lobotomize and kill people for their sexual preferences or gender?

Because allowing for variance meant accepting inefficiency.

Europa's elite had outlawed homosexuality because it meant that human components within their society were not performing to the needs and roles of that organism. Society, a constructed creature of the Dame family and its kin. Society demanded more components, more humans, more, more; greedy, hungry Society. Gay females could still reproduce and provide more components for the Society if they were kept alive and forced to conform; lobotomized, bound, why waste resources? Females were always resources. One male could impregnate many females and still produce components for Society. So. Gay males were killed because they were surplus. Females were not. Simple. Brutal. Efficient. If you rebelled, you were a defective portion of society and would be culled.

If you examined it, you saw the whirring mechanisms of a never-ending system. More components, always. More, more, more. If the population ever dropped or remained stable, this society's economic models would falter.

That was all it was.

Efficiency.

There was no respect for life, for consciousness, for the individual will. The wealthy had constructed this Society to serve their needs, turning humans into components, mattering no more than seabed metals or water or silk. Society would not die or change unless it served their needs. Their fondest wish, above all, was to remain in power forever. How human. The desire to never change. Never adapt.

Insanity.

Efficiency.

I shivered.

I used to think it was impossible for those two concepts to co-exist. What did that mean about the hyper-efficient Fisherman I'd been before the humans took my skin and stranded me in this scrap of flesh?

Maybe I was more human than I'd thought.

"I gotta find Isobel before we leave," Liore said, standing.

Streaks of viscera daubed her body. A tatter of skin dangled from her hair. I tried the radio again.

Nothing but static.

We trudged to the lunchroom. There was longer any reason to run. Whatever waited would eventually find us.

Isobel's body did not appear along the way.

One pair of swinging plastic doors guarded the lunchroom entrance. Square plexiglass windows offered a glimpse. Normally, scratches and scuffs clouded them.

Today, a thin sheet of blood reddened each window. From the gap between door and ground, blood oozed. It reeked of metal and salt. Thick enough to tickle the back of my throat. Under that, fecal matter.

Liore reached down, ran her fingers through the blood puddle, and lapped it off. She smiled. Not a passionate grin—a content, mildly amused smile. The Bad Humans were dead. She was not. The Bad Humans had jammed a metal stick into her frontal lobe and told her to count down from ten, and jiggled the stick until she could no longer count. The Bad Humans who were called Auntie and Baba, watched in silence.

Ten.

Nine.

Eight.

(*eight, what comes after—*)

Seven.

(*seven then five, no, sex, no...six....no....*)

S-six...

(*...no...*)

Twitch of the lips. Was that an f for five? Keep jiggling.

(*......*)

(*......*)

But now the Bad Humans lie dead. Harmless. Their blood tasted like rich honey on her tongue. She would sup, laugh, slip into the water (*lovely, lovely home*), happy, beyond where anyone could hurt her. Isobel was a Bad Human—a Very Bad Human—but Liore would find her soon and then there would be no more Isobel.

Where did Isobel's body go?

Of course, Liore Hyung smiled.

I smiled, too.

I scooped up blood and drank alongside her. Then I nudged the lunchroom door open.

Thirty-one dead crewmen bled, piled in a pyramid atop the lunchroom table. Near the apex, Cherise's body spasmed, blood gushing from a speared eye socket. Captain Anderson lay akimbo at the top. Red matter filled both his eye sockets.

Three handguns lay scattered on the blood-splattered floor. Exposed steel shined in corkscrew patterns along the blue-painted walls, where bullets had ricocheted and taken off paint. Waxed paper gum wrappers, floating in blood, reflected pink in it. In the reflections, those half-crumpled wrappers looked like bits of small intestine. Blood trickled off the table.

Fecal matter, iron, sulfurous gunpowder.

My nose wrinkled.

Overhead lights blazed . Ceiling air vents chuffed. Liore

rubbed her palms together, mouth still rouged in blood. The hem of my silk gown glistened red. Red, red, red. It lined grooves in my hands.

"We should look distressed," I said softly. "The cameras are still watching."

"No," Liore said.

"Go Home. I need to find who killed them."

"Not till I find Isobel—"

"It wasn't Isobel's fault they hurt you."

Liore bared her teeth. "She let it—"

Electricity flooded the air.

Invisible needles prickled my scalp. Crackling noises came from two spots near the ceiling. Wisps of smoke rose.

Then it was over, and Dame Isobel's voice came from the kitchen. "Get in here."

Isobel?

I froze.

Liore bolted for the kitchen door. She crashed through, one hip forward—

A tentacle scooped her up by the waist and dragged her in.

Thunk!

Not feeling my legs, I ventured into the kitchen. Here they were. The other Fisherman. At last, an explanation for—

Two Isobels stood in the kitchen. Liore struggled against the wall, over the sink, bound in a wad of clear, glue-like substance. She partially dissolved, stopped, and formed back into human, cursing.

I blinked.

There were still two Isobels.

One of them wore her standard glittering opals, curled pale hair, and blue floor-length gown. Blood gloved her forearms, dripping on the floor. The other Isobel stood expressionless, without makeup, clad in a crew jumpsuit.

No.

Too much. Too many abnormal events.

No more.

I threw up my hands, turned on my heel, and started for the door.

"Stay here," the gowned Isobel said.

I continued towards the door.

"Please," the gowned Isobel said.

That one must be the other Fisherman. Human Isobel would be screaming those words at me.

"If you don't stay, I'll make you," said not-Isobel.

Slick muscle dragged down the back of my neck. Mucous itched where it touched.

(you)

(YOU!)

Recognition sparked.

And tears filled my eyes.

My Friend.

This was My Friend. My closest companion. Or so I'd thought. They'd engineered this conspiracy, watched me suffer for three weeks, and allowed me to be seen as a monster for deeds I hadn't done. Clearly, they did not feel as I felt towards them.

I kept my tone level, but tears dribbled down both cheeks. "You watched them rip off my skin and did nothing?"

"Necessary."

"How so?"

"You act as if I ordered this or endangered you," my Friend said.

"I never would've done any of this to you."

"We know. That's why we used you," Friend said.

"Used me?"

"Aeter's plan. They required you show everyone how to grow new skins. Aeter bestowed the ability on us."

"You let them hurt me," I said, voice breaking.

"I'm sorry."

The Isobel in the jumpsuit went to Liore, paling. Liore lunged at her. Couldn't reach. Her teeth clicked together on air.

"Liore. I love you," Isobel said, "Liore—"

Liore spat. A gob of whitish saliva landed between Isobel's eyebrows.

Isobel's lip curled. She scrubbed the spit off her face.

"You turned her into a feral *fucking alien?*" Isobel snapped.

"Aeter did," Friend said.

"That wasn't what I asked for. I played my role. Change her back to human."

"Aeter won't."

Isobel's jaw muscles worked, jumping under her skin.

"She's a disgusting fucking alien now? I'm supposed to—"

Feral. Alien.

So much disgust it made my stomach lurch; the contempt in Isobel's lifted upper lip, how one of her eyes scrunched up tighter than the other, the quick downward twitching of her mouth, exposing dry teeth. No saliva was left in her mouth. Visceral disgust.

Heartbeats pounded through my stomach as if it'd slipped into my innards.

Disgusting.

Alien.

Had I ever interacted with the real Dame Isobel? Not a literal statement, since I had interacted with human Isobel, but...

"We had sexual intercourse," I said.

She whirled to face me, lip still curled. "What are you still doing here, Fisherman? Go home. I peeled your skin off, kept you occupied, babysat you, and you grew it back. You're done. Now, go share that knowledge with the other Fishermen and make Aeter happy."

Through my numb brain, I managed, "I thought you enjoyed it."

"We had fun. We fucked. That's it."

"You constantly complained I wasn't attached to you."

"If I didn't play the role of love-struck, crazy Isobel, everyone would've wondered why I was keeping you aboard the ship," she snapped.

Why was I still crying?

"Y-you said you loved me," I said.

"That wasn't me."

"What actually happened, Isobel?"

Dame Isobel shook her head. "You Fishermen. Always needing to *know* everything."

Then she told me.

CHAPTER 9

Isobel's Tale.

Fumbling hands, both sets. Secret kisses behind the magnolia tree, in a garden that never stops flowering. You taste menthol at the back of her mouth. Four siblings and a dying set of grandparents weigh her thoughts down. Your fingers grope lower into her leggings; you already breached her bleak green housekeeper's smock, crinkled from use, discarded like a limp snakeskin beneath rosebushes. Roses blaze blue as the artificially projected sky overhead. Robotic butterflies flit in circular patterns. Too perfect. Tell the programmers later—they'll adjust the settings.

Her nipples harden through her camisole.

You say, "Relax, Lee..."

"Liore," she purrs.

Liore. That's her name. Liore. Remember it. This one shifts her hips forward, into your fingers. Thumb on her clit, slow circles; inside you, trailing glitter stars. Slippery wetness. She bucks in rhythm to your hand until her walls contract around your finger, *squeeze-squeeze-squeeze*, and she moans. Soft enough to be an exhale.

You retreat.

"We only have fifteen minutes before my shift starts," she says.

You lap her off your fingers—tangy, faintly metallic.

She asks, "When did you know?"

Your face burns. "It's just fun. It doesn't mean anything."

"You could make a difference, Isobel."

"I'm not some—"

"Not what?" Liore says, too quietly.

"Fine. Okay. My thirteenth birthday party. The non-public one. I had some friends over. Not real friends. You don't have real friends when you're this rich. All we ever did was brag about our families and backstab each other," you say, staring at the blue flowers, "The Gariellus twins, Magda and Maeve, said I'd marry their little brother, Paloma. We had my cousin, Theo, Theophania, along even though she was eight. Then we had bratty Sano Anastasia. God, the Sano family burns through money. Anyway, we were all in my room with Celia, giggling over a tray of flayed squid hearts and salmon canapes and the non-alcoholic champagne fizzing in our flute glasses—"

"Isobel."

You chew your lip. "I'm getting to it. I argued with the twins, said I'd never marry their brother. Anastasia said the only way we'd settle it was by playing a game. We agreed. She turned on the TV and put it to this psychic algorithm channel with glittery font, pink hearts, Cupids, and a timer going in the upper corner. Pay-per-minute. You put your hands on the TV screen, and it'd take your vitals, play some images, and tell you about your best future husband by generating an image of him. It didn't have the capacity to measure vitals, but we thought it sounded fun. Why not? We had money to burn."

You breathe. The next part aches as it comes out.

"These girls…they acted like bizarro aliens when the TV showed their 'dream guy'. 'Ooh, look at him!' 'He's tall!' 'Ana, look at yours, he has abs,' but the men looked the same to me. I didn't get what they saw. Then it was my turn, and the program generated an image of a blond swimmer athlete type, said he'd be intelligent. A bookworm with abs. Everyone squealed, and I just…stood there, not knowing what I was supposed to be feeling. It didn't matter. We all knew our parents would be arranging our marriages in a few years. I thought I was better than Ana and the twins. Smarter. I knew not to get attached to a man."

Liore touches your arm. "And then there was a girl, and she made you feel like you carried sunlight in your belly."

"Laundry girl. We were both fifteen. Celia caught us kissing."

"What happened to her?"

A mechanical blue Morpho butterfly settles on the smock. Its actuators drone. Fake honeybees buzz among the tiger lilies.

"They sent her away," you say.

That's all you say.

YOUR MOTHER CALLS you into the parlor a month later and dismisses the servants for the rest of the evening. A paid break, she tells them. She wastes no time composing a lie. She doesn't sour the statement with a fake smile. Admirable, really. The servants leave.

"Shut the door behind you," she says.

You do.

Here she sits on the silk couch, wearing nothing but a top, tumbler of absinthe in her spidery hand, colorless mouth twitching. Gray pubes seethe atop her cunt. Age spots barnacle her hips and thighs.

"You think I wanted to fuck your father, Isobel?"

She jabs a thumb at the portrait looming over the couch. Your parents look like a set of cave fish in that one, those eyeless translucent cave-things.

Your mother rasps, "Answer me."

"No," you say.

The colorless gray mouth jerks down. It might be a sneer. She pats the seat next to her. You don't move.

"I didn't, but I was married to him. You understand that concept. We have responsibilities that others don't. Did you pick one of the matches out?"

"They won't prosecute me," you say.

Your mother sips her absinthe. Her breath washes over you. Alcohol and cooked salmon.

"Correct. They won't prosecute you. They'll prosecute *her*," she says, shaking her head. "But you didn't care about the last two, either."

"Nothing bad really happened," you say.

"Jana can't get a job anywhere besides the waste processing plant, because she's a felon. Lily took a nice vacation at a nice facility with straps on the chairs."

"I don't know what you're talking about, Mother."

"You never could be taught to lie. The instructors said you didn't need it. You were always a natural."

She smiles at you, showing no teeth. Her chin is sinking into her shoulders, neck melting. The corners of her mouth droop hideously. Your mother, the anglerfish. The hair left on her scalp could fit between two fingers.

Your mother is the only person who sees what you really are.

"I won't bribe the authorities again," she says. "When they catch you, I'll make you watch the punishment. You need to learn responsibility."

"You shouldn't drink so much, Mother. It's making you incoherent."

"If you fire Liore Hyung tomorrow, nothing will happen. Pick your match from the selected husbands, fire her, quit your girl-hunting, and everyone will be fine."

"I can't have fun?"

"Stop playing with breakable toys, Isobel."

She slumps back, waves a hand at the door. You're dismissed.

Is it really that terrible to want something fun?

You weigh yourself every day. Servants pluck hairs from your brows, lips, and wax you every day. A skilled lady from a Martian colony brushes cosmetics onto your face. Your nose has deviated two millimeters to the left over the last twelve months. In three months, you'll have them schedule your fifth nose job to realign the cartilage. Facial implants massage you while you sleep to stimulate collagen production. Wrinkles have appeared, and you're only twenty-three. No time to waste. Seventeen products compose your skin regimen.

Mother thinks it's all stupid. You know better. Pretty Dame Isobel is a doll for the masses to covet, a princess smiling from her tower. Pomp and circumstance give the illusion of importance.

Soon your flesh will settle and liquify like hers, and you'll be a monster. Mother enjoys herself still. Why? She's hideous.

Too soon, too soon.

Then oblivion.

You get so tired of dreading death you decide to kill yourself. You fail. Try again. Fail again. They put in implants so you can't.

Life is inevitable, Isobel, Celia comforts, when she catches you examining your face for sebaceous filaments.

You almost snarl, *Not when you're worth billions, it fucking isn't.*

Ethereal model Isobel. That's you. Her doll's eyes sparkle with life—because of the eyedrops you use. Her waist tapers sharply. She's statuesque—because of the steel and bone implants embedded in your femurs.

Dame Isobel, jewel of Europa.

Liore brings you to her home for dinner, and nobody recognizes you.

Without your cosmetics, jewels, and gowns, you're only a pretty pale-haired girl. Liore's little sister asks if you always speak with your mouth full. Dumpling balanced on your soup spoon, you chew, swallow, try not to cry.

I'm...nothing.

"Bell's from my biotech intro class," Liore says, grinning. "She works down La Sirena. You still gunning for that sweet front desk position, Bell?"

You try not to look at your disgusting drab pants and gray shirt. Dishwater gray, everything is. Crooked seams zigzag along the hems.

"Yes," you manage.

Liore's aunt and uncle have raised her and the other four siblings after the airlock accident killed Liore's mother. Liore's father had disappeared a few months before. Someone found his severed head in a garbage can outside of a nightclub, mouth stuffed full of yellow debt receipts and medical bills.

"What do you like to do outside of work, Bell?" Auntie asks.

Try not to think about how I'm turning into a disgusting decrepit monster with every passing second.

Liore's auntie weighs about three hundred pounds and all of it's on her stomach. Her perpetually red hands crack and bleed from years of exposure to cleaning chemicals. Liore's Baba is poker-thin, stubby, a little man with dark skin and penetrating eyes. Clips restrain his curly hair back in a knot at the base of his skull.

"Sometimes I like to go to Madison Garden," you say.

"Oh, that's a pretty one. I knew the guy who designed the pink butterflies there, I ever tell you that, Liore? Used to clean his mansion. Beautiful mansion. Three kitchens. Can you believe that? No kids. Three kitchens," Auntie rasps.

"That's nice," you say.

This comedy of errors continues throughout the evening.

Before you sneak back home, Liore nudges you. She holds a pink slip of paper.

"There's a few openings for an apprentice on the EMS 001-TXS. It's a mining rig. They go to the South Pole for six months per run. Ship leaves in two weeks. Pay's not bad. People don't care what you do in your free time on a mining rig."

Your heart jitters. Your mouth goes sticky and dry.

"You're leaving me?" you ask.

Liore waggles her tongue at you. "Isobel, you sweet, naive gal. I'm saying we both get jobs on the mining rig."

"Excuse me?"

"You could get forged documents tomorrow if you wanted to. You wanna stop being Dame Isobel, you can. We can be together."

"There'll be a manhunt for me."

"Please. Your mother hates you."

"Everyone will scour Brilliante's camera footage for me."

"Get a face-blocker like all the other rich people do when they go out clubbing," Liore says. "Easy-peasy. Then you'll be on a ship at the South Pole, in the middle of nowhere, for six months. By the time you come back, you'll be a disappeared person."

Disappeared.

No skin products on that mining rig. The work will ruin your hands, hair, and skin. Someone will hack your long, beautiful hair off while you're sleeping. Instead of fading into an invisible worthless monster over the course of a few decades…

Fuck that.

"Sure, I'll think about it," you tell Liore.

Her smile falls. She turns away. You grab her rough hand,

yank her back, and press your lips to hers. Taste the menthol, the salt, in her saliva. She kisses back.

"I love you," she says.

You can't look at her. "I love you too."

You head back home.

That's the last time you see her until the lobotomy.

THE VIDEO CAMERAS at the bus stop caught you and Liore kissing. Mother tells you later. Clear as diamonds, the footage is.

You're Dame Isobel, so nothing happens.

She's a housekeeper from a long line of lower-class scum, but it's her first offense, so they won't kill her. The nice judge with the pinched nostrils and grey hair says that part delicately. Liore Hyung can be reformed. She has two options. Go to a sexual healing clinic, such as LUV, or a frontal lobotomy.

The clinics reject her application, because she can't afford it. Doesn't meet the criteria for a payment plan. You pay them. Twice what they're owed. Suddenly, she's accepted.

But as she's packing to go, more footage comes out.

Liore Hyung, engaging a female prostitute in oral sex.

Liore Hyung, staring right at the camera, kissing another housekeeper.

The next hearing goes quickly.

Lobotomy, or execution.

Liore chooses execution. Her auntie has her declared mentally incompetent—attempting to have the sentence turned over entirely—and goes for the lobotomy. Because the brain can heal. At least Liore won't be dead. Maybe it won't work. Sometimes they don't.

You wish you could tell Auntie that Liore's better off dead.

Liore shows up in your dreams, hissing, "Isobel. Isobel. Say something. Isobel."

You bolt awake every time, dry heaving.

Monster.

They can't know I'm a monster.

Thin streams of spit ooze out of your mouth and onto the bed. No vomit. You haven't eaten anything in the last two days. Three pimples blight your jawline from stress.

Isobel. Isobel.

Monster.

You pay an escape crew to break Liore out of prison and smuggle her onto a mining rig. They reach the docks before the first gunshots ring out. Crew ditches Liore and runs. Liore's lobotomy gets moved to tomorrow morning.

You have every last one of them killed.

Mother laughs when she catches you with the proof of death pictures. These snipers did a better job than the escape crew. Maybe the crew should take a lesson from them.

Oh, wait. They can't.

They're all dead.

TWELVE HOURS UNTIL THE LOBOTOMY.

So Liore has to be there, but does it have to actually be Liore? No. All you need to find is someone who can look like Liore, who can take the punishment instead of her. Luckily, there's something living on Europa that can do it. Easily. One of the Fishermen. You've got twelve hours to find one and infinite money to do it with.

You read old legends until you see colors out the corner of your eyes; blue bits of light.

Every kid on Europa goes through that phase where they think Fishermen are the coolest thing ever, and you weren't any different. Mysterious aliens under the water? They can look like anything? Whoa, they took down a whole sea-fighter? Just ate it in one gulp. Why don't they talk to us?

Stories say the Fishermen can heal from anything.

Some first-hand accounts:

Twenty-two years ago—unnamed woman hears something say *Aeter,* while she's in an induced coma. Has vivid dreams about swimming below the ice. Upon reviving, she knows the precise locations of several classified underwater storage sites.

Fifty years ago—Reece is on a mining expedition when a massive tentacled abomination cracks a hole in the ice, sticks its head out, and forms into a copy of him. It beckons him from the ice. A naked man. When it sees he isn't coming, it slips back into the water.

One-hundred years ago—The Arlington Expedition captures an aquatic alien lifeform that appears to be a primitive "mermaid". They drug it and begin dissecting it. The alien sprouts tentacles, throttling everyone in the operating room to death instantaneously. While Yeoman, the makeshift nurse, cowers in a corner, the alien touches his arm and forms into a copy of him. *I left you alive as a warning. Don't bother us again,* it says, in a flat voice. It consumes the cadavers in front of Yeoman. Then it forms into a monstrous shape and dives overboard. Yeoman names it a Fisherman, to minimize the horror.

They can heal. They can look like anyone.

You contact Europa's self-proclaimed 'expert scientist' on

Fishermen and offer him anything he wants if he can find one for you.

"Sure. Give me a few months, a trawling ship, and a—"

"I need one in twelve hours or less," you say.

The scientist laughs.

You grit your teeth. "What will it take?"

"It's impossible, Dame Isobel. They're always moving, there's maybe a thousand of them in existence, and they don't like humans."

You try to slice your wrists open later. Safety wires emerge. Champagne fills your gullet and fogs your mind into fizzy oblivion.

THE STENCH OF RUBBING ALCOHOL. A female doctor with vulpine cheekbones and blood-red lipstick eases the lobotomy pick into Liore's tear duct. Liore blinks sluggishly, pupils pinpricks, tongue purple from the grape-flavored sedative they made her swallow.

Doctor wiggles the pick. Says, *Count down out loud, Miss Hyung.*

Ten.

Nine.

E-eight.

Liore's lips struggle. She swallows.

S-seven.

Vomit fills your mouth, acidic and sweet. Bits of egg and maple syrup and curdled milk. You spew it on the floor.

S-six.

Liore, you're making it up, you're not really forgetting what comes next—

Her lips form a *f.*

The doctor stops. Squints. *Miss Hyung, can you remember what comes before six?*

Liore's gaze is blank. Unfocused.

Doctor removes the pick. Mucous slimes the end. Liore tries to stand and stumbles. Auntie and Baba catch her. Baba's red-rimmed eyes look like a demon's.

Thank god I'm behind the mirror. They would kill me.

You can't move. You don't. Five minutes after they've taken Liore away, Celia tugs you back through the hallway and into your chauffeured car.

YOU CONTACT that scientist after your hangover's gone. You weigh seven pounds less this week. Two pustules fester on your chin. Even the cosmetic lady can't cover them.

You've gone crazy, Isobel, Mother says.

You can't do it, Isobel.

Isobel! Pick a husband and put it out of your head.

She says the guilt goes away if you ignore it, but it's a risk you can't take.

ten-nine-eight—

No.

Don't think about it.

"Dame Isobel? Are you listening?" the scientist asks, over the phone.

"You said they have a god?"

"It's their progenitor."

"Do you think it can heal people, like the coma case from twenty years ago?"

"There's no evidence," he says.

You argue for a few minutes before getting to the meat of it: How would someone go on an expedition to talk to a Fisherman?

You ask, "You said the South Pole, around this time of year?"

"If I may…having an expert aboard your ship might help your expedition—"

"I need knowledge to barter?"

"Technically, yes, but you *have* knowledge they want. Humans are new to Europa. Let one of them mimic you, and it will tell you anything you want to know. That's assuming you make contact."

"I need a mining rig or a trawler?"

"Um, yes, but it may be difficult…even if you follow their migration pattern, they aren't going to approach a ship unless you give them a reason…you might have to provoke them by releasing something into the ocean."

"That's the most effective option?"

"If you're lucky, one of them will form vocal cords and tell you to stop. If you're unlucky…they might, uh, just decide to get rid of the problem. It's happened a few times."

"Three times in a hundred years."

"I'll do anything to come. You don't have to pay me. I'll work for free, I'll even—"

"Maybe next time. I'll fund your research for the next five years as a thank-you. I appreciate your time," you say robotically. "The money will be wired to your research account tomorrow. Thank you. Good-bye."

See, here's the thing. If *you* were a Fisherman, you'd form into a human and walk around somewhere to collect free knowledge. This scientist is saying they don't. Why not? Either this scientist doesn't know as much as he thinks he does, or Fishermen *do* walk around as humans. You just have to catch one doing it.

You send someone to search hospital records. Are there any unnamed people, maybe seeming lost? People without names?

Look for a combination of cold logic and naivety.

Records turn up a few homeless schizophrenics, nothing more.

Hm.

Mining rig goes to the South Pole, six months, Liore whispers.

You make some phone calls to have other people make phone calls to the Dame Family's mining divisions. The Dame family specializes in gold and silicon. Thirty mining rigs travel Europa, breaking ice along the way. Within that sphere, fifteen hundred staff are employed by the Dame Family—crewmen, miners, cooks, support crew, security officers.

"Make a list of everyone who's gone on an expedition to the South Pole in the last year, and who have had recorded 'abnormal behavior' in the last twelve months, emphasis on memory loss, confusion, and antisocial behavior," you command.

Mother says you're crazy. Why correct her?

You outfit the ENS *Princess* for an expedition to the South Pole.

Thirty-five names come up positive.

You make the sudden expedition public and offer all thirty-five 'abnormal' crewmen twice their usual pay to go on this little six-week voyage of yours. You, the pretty and wealthy princess, will be on the ship. Let them dream about falling in love with you and marrying you.

Three of them turn the job offer down. You investigate: one lost his child two weeks ago (hence the abnormal behavior), one is ninety-three years young and going crazy from dementia, and the third simply wants to nurture his heroin addiction in a nice dark crack den until it kills him. Understandable.

Managerial staff interview the thirty-two remaining potentials, videotaping the interviews at your request. You analyze the footage, looking for...something. Fins? Gills? Creepy eyes? Don't know what. You'll know it when you see it.

And see it, you do.

Interview #17: Security officer Gavin LaBeouf slithers into the interview chair—*he's just walking, get a grip*—and tries to smile. His lips pull back from his teeth and ooze down too quickly again.

Your scalp prickles.

Not right.

A thread of nausea tickles the back of your throat.

Gavin LaBeouf says he doesn't have any family. He lives alone. According to your paperwork, he has two children and a wife.

He blinks too slowly, like a lizard.

Holy fuck. Fuck. I actually have one sitting in that office.

You do think for a split second: *I could make millions if I captured "Gavin" and made it talk.*

You wouldn't. You don't care about money right now.

You're a bad person masquerading as a princess, Isobel, Mother says, *Stop pretending.*

"Shut up, Mother," you whisper.

With your blessing, "Gavin LaBeouf" becomes the Head Security Officer aboard the ENS *Princess*.

THE WORST PART of it is, you end up telling "Gavin" everything. Not even a week into the voyage, and you're crying into its chest. His chest. Whatever.

You had better plans.

Figures.

Gavin guards you every time you're outside your cabin. In the interview, all you could see were his inhuman little twitches and slow blinks. In person, he still does them, but there's a warmth to it because there's no self-consciousness. Gavin listens when others speak. His gaze tracks every movement, fascinated. It's almost charming.

Everyone else thinks he's got neurological damage, or he's on drugs.

So you get drunker than drunk, lukewarm champagne bottle in each hand, slumped against the wall outside your cabin.

Ten.

Nine.

Eight—

"Make it stop," you bleat, "Make it stop make it—"

"Dame Isobel?" Gavin says.

He's appeared out of thin fucking air, it feels like.

And that's when you stupidly say, slurring, "Make your god heal Liore. I know you can talk to it. That's what the legends say."

Gavin stops blinking. He studies you.

"I think you need to go to bed," he says.

"I know you're a Fisherman."

"You've had a lot of ethanol alcohol, Dame Isobel."

"See, humans don't call it 'ethanol'," you say. "You aren't as good as you think you are. Talk to me. This entire voyage was so I could find a Fisherman and get Liore Hyung healed."

Gavin gets you to a standing position. "You should go to bed. Inside."

"Talk to me. Why are you here?"

He enters the passcode for the white carved door. It beeps, clicks, and slides open.

"Where's Celia?" Gavin asks.

"I didn't want her to see me like this."

The door shuts with a soft *snap*.

"She's gone?"

"There aren't any cameras in here, either," you say.

He could kill you right now and get away with it.

"You sound like you're struggling," he says.

Drunk, you collapse onto your bed and sob. Gavin awkwardly hugs you. That's the real sign he's a Fisherman. No human would be dumb enough to try hugging Dame Isobel, the jewel of Europa, especially not some low-grade security officer on a mining rig.

He hugs you like you're an ice sculpture he doesn't want to melt. Snuffling, you cry into his chest. Snot and tears seep into his jumpsuit.

You tell him everything.

About being gay. About the other girls. Liore. Trying to save Liore. Reading the legends, calling the scientist. Being forced to watch her get the lobotomy. The guilt. Going crazy. Deciding to find a Fisherman.

You even tell him about watching his interview footage, knowing he isn't human.

Through the whole sad fucking story, Gavin just kind of pats your head and lets you cry. Bottles of lemon-cucumber water chill in a bucket of ice on the far bedside table. Your throat's scratchy from crying. Condensation weeps down the metal bucket.

You start to untangle yourself so you can get the water.

Gavin lazily reaches for it.

His arm lengthens and twists into a tentacle. It grabs a water, retracts, and then shapes back into human. Fingers split off. Hairs sprout.

It sobers you immediately.

He hands you the water. "You're dehydrated."

"Thanks."

You sip. Gavin begins his spiel.

Between sips, all you can think is, *I'm doing something that nobody's ever done, in a hundred years of trying. I'm talking to a Fisherman.*

The Fishermen's creator-god goes by Aeter. Ate-er. Rhymes with *Ate her.*

"Aeter's allowing me to tell you everything…Aeter's talking to me right now. Which means Aeter's amused by…this. By you.

Aeter does what Aeter wants, Dame Isobel. I don't know how this situation will end for you," Gavin says.

You snort. "I could die. Yeah. I've wanted that since I was twelve."

"There are worse things than having your existence end."

"I know."

"Aeter could reach into your mind and turn you into a tubeworm."

"So healing Liore's brain damage should be pretty fucking easy for Aeter to do."

The ship jolts.

You tense. Gavin purses his lips into a line.

"I don't know how this situation will end for you, Dame Isobel," he says.

Gavin continues. He's pretending to be human because Aeter wants to give the Fishermen a new ability and spread the knowledge. In order to do that, one of them needs to regrow their 'skin' in a stressful situation, with no knowledge. His job is to board a mining rig, integrate with the human crewmen, and find a way to capture another Fisherman. He'll peel off their 'skin', imprison them, and wait for the 2-3 weeks it'll take to regrow another skin.

"I'm there to ensure no actual harm comes to the other Fisherman," he says.

He stops blinking again. For two minutes, he sits without blinking or speaking.

"You're stressed out," you say.

"I have to hurt a…companion. A friend. My closest companion. There's only one Fisherman who can do this adequately. They're very passive. Anyone else would steal a knife or sharp object and go on a massacre to get their skin back, instead of waiting long enough for their skin to regrow. I don't like having to hurt my…friend."

"Only for a few weeks," you say.

"I don't like it. I will do it, because Aeter wants me to, but I wish I could avoid this. I want to go home."

"I'll make sure everything goes according to plan. Believe me, I can act. In return, Aeter's gonna heal Liore Hyung. Gavin—can I call you Gavin? Do you have a real name?"

"'Gavin' is adequate."

You look directly at him. "As a personal favor—when all of this is done, will you kill me?"

"Why?"

"I can't live with the guilt."

"That statement is inaccurate. You are currently living."

"No. I'm not."

"You can kill yourself without physically harming your body, Dame Isobel. I would help you find a job on a mining rig. Vanish. Create a new identity."

"I can't."

"Why?"

Because I'll liquify into a monster, age, and die.

Because I'll be the jewel of Europa, whether I'm alive or dead. I will not be lower-class scum. I will not be an ugly, worthless monster.

"You wouldn't understand," you say.

Yes, you fuck Fisherman.

Is having fun such a terrible thing?

See, Mother. I learned. I found a toy that won't break.

In that second, before the last of her skin rips off, Fisherman puts a tentacle to your skin and mimics you. Fisherman's face doesn't turn out right, but she doesn't know it. It's almost cute. Her nose melds into her cheeks. Her mouth's twisted.

You keep her on edge for two weeks. Here's crazy Isobel. Here's Isobel in love, Fisherman. Silly Fisherman.

You gaslight her for two weeks.

By pretending to know nothing about Aeter, you keep her angry enough to not question more. It's a fine balance—angry and irritated, but not murderous. Stupidly, you demand *wishes* from Aeter. Fine. Aeter's already got Their many millions of eyes locked on *you*. Why not go for broke? Aeter, make Paloma dead, too. Aeter, could you just wreck the whole Dame Family for me? I hate all of this.

You could've sworn something whispered back, voice mocking: *But you're the jewel of Europa, Isobel.*

Gavin almost gives everything away when he mentions Liore in front of Fisherman. You almost snap.

You're fired, Gavin, you warn.

That's your code phrase for, *I'm about to give up. Stop it.*

In case of an emergency, Gavin's is, *I'm quitting, Dame Isobel.*

Things go as planned until Gavin rushes to your room, palm-sized video screen between his fingers, and says, "There's another outside."

"What?"

"Fisherman saw. I had to sedate her."

You slam your wine glass down. "Why is there another one outside?"

"I don't know them," he says.

He trembles. The yellow beads in his beard shake.

"We all know each other," he says. "Fisherman's talking to them right now. I got the captain to think there wasn't anything. It was easy. He's on cocaine."

"Fucking Anderson and his drugs."

"Fisherman doesn't know who it is, either. I'm watching the video footage right now."

"Okay, isn't her skin pretty much done growing?"

"Needs another day or two."

"So, another day or two. We'll make time."

"Isobel, are you aware of the video camera hidden by your bed?"

"Mother's always watching me. Maybe she likes to watch. I had to get the gay from someone in my family, after all," you say, and raise your voice. "Mother, do you like it?"

"You're acting irrational, Isobel."

"Yeah, so here's what that camera means. My mother's finally gonna pull the trigger and have me killed. Probably in this room. Footage will be proof of death. I'd know. I've had people killed. Good riddance. I don't know who the assassin is," you say.

Gavin takes the wine glass from your hand. He hugs you.

"I'm sorry you're suffering," he says.

"Fuck you. Give me my wine back."

"Your attempt to isolate yourself will not work. I have become aware of human psychology. You are attempting self-destruction."

"God-fucking-dammit, Gavin. Let me die."

"I will not."

"Why? I'm only one human. A shitty one, too. I'm vain, I'm careless, and I'd die before I gave up my privilege, and I know how selfish that is."

And then you bawl again, crying so hard you dry-heave. Celia comes in, sees you and Gavin, and backs out of the room. Celia's hoping you finally found a man; she'll let you be inappropriate with one, even if he's lower class.

"My nose's twisted five millimeters to the left since my last nose job. I made a new wrinkle on my forehead," you recite, "Twenty sebaceous filaments festering on my nose."

Gavin sighs. "How will we make more time for Fisherman?"

"Is the other one going to destroy the ship?"

"No. I think they're interested."

"Ignore them, then."

"The crew's trying to mutiny."

"Fine."

"Isobel, if there's violence and they shoot me, I will not stay dead. They'll know what I am."

"Okay…why can't you stay dead?" you ask.

"Because I—"

"Sorry, rhetorical question. You could keep yourself alive but looking dead, right? Heal your body just enough to stay alive? Or mutate in a way that can't be seen from the outside?"

"Mmmmm…. yes."

"All we have to do is make the entire crew paranoid about Fisherman. That'll stop the mutiny until her skin grows."

"What's your plan?"

"I'll kill you, frame Fisherman for your death, and put her in the brig for a few days. All you have to do is hide in the morgue. Easy."

It almost works.

But Anderson plays detective, realizes that Fisherman's not to blame, and the whole thing goes rapidly to shit when they all put together that *Gavin's* a Fisherman. Gavin panics. What if they take off his skin? Put him in the brig and hurt him the way they hurt Fisherman?

You're both hiding in your closet behind the racks of clothes.

Gavin has stopped blinking. A tentacle darts out of his mouth, extends, and retracts. In. Out. In. Out. Besides that, he's utterly still.

You put an arm around him and hold him close.

"Okay, okay," you say. "Here's the thing about humans. We hate feeling like we're nothing. Even if they catch you, all you have to do is make them feel valuable. Say that you pretended to be Gavin because you liked them. You were fascinated by them. Humans love hearing that. Everyone on this ship hates Fisherman, because she's weird and doesn't even try talking to them. You're just Gavin. They think you're on drugs, but you're still a person. If you said that Fisherman came aboard to hurt you, they might even believe it."

He nods. He starts blinking.

"Fisherman's skin grew back faster than we thought. She's figuring it out. Gavin, we did everything we needed to. The rest will figure itself out. Okay?"

"Okay."

"Now, you're going to fry those video cameras and take my form. Celia's going to come back here. Go with her. Keep her distracted. While you do that, I'll find Fisherman and tell her the truth."

"She might hurt you."

"No. Because she loves me," you say bitterly. "I made her love me. What a human being I am."

He laughs under his breath. It's not real laughter. Too sad and soft.

Still.

You've never heard him laugh before.

"I'm the one who peeled her skin off. What a Fisherman I am," Gavin says.

"I'm sorry you had to hurt your only friend."

"That statement is inaccurate. Fisherman is not my only friend anymore. I have you, too."

"Gavin…"

And the sudden shame of what you *really are* makes your eyes burn.

Dame Isobel, jewel of Europa.

We never could teach you to lie, Isobel. You were a natural. The instructors said so.

Isobel. Isobel.

Seventeen skin products, five nose jobs, weight maintained within five pounds, hair always curled and glittered with opals, Dame Isobel, jewel of Europa; doll in a high tower; the fairytale princess killing her failed suitors—you destroyed their lives, you as good as killed them—

Scared to become a monster? Why?

I've always been a monster.

You wipe the tears away before Gavin sees them.

"Thank you. For being my friend. I've never had a real friend before," you say.

He mimics your form and waits on the bed for Celia. You pause, stuffed into the back of the closet, smothered in your fine gowns.

Monster in a ten-thousand-dollar gown.

You change into one of Fisherman's discarded jumpsuits before you leave, both hands fumbling.

CHAPTER 10

S o.

Apparently, I was a passive idiot and had always been.

I turned to my Friend, 'Gavin', who had shifted back into the Gavin form and thrown on a jumpsuit while Isobel spoke. Gavin towered over everyone else.

"You and Aeter think so highly of me," I said.

"I meant 'efficient', not passive. You won't cause a bloodbath if there doesn't need to be one—"

"Why did you kill the remaining crewmen?" I asked.

Isobel shook her head. "We didn't."

"Gavin?"

His/their eyelids fluttered. I saw him remember to blink.

"I went into the lunchroom after you killed Celia, still looking like Isobel. I had plans to reassure the crewmen as Isobel, letting them know the Fishermen were off the boat, so we would go home immediately," he said.

"They didn't believe you, so you massacred them," I said.

Gavin produced a pocket-sized video screen. He fiddled with it.

"I'm a disgusting alien, Isobel?" Gavin muttered.

She looked greyish-white under the kitchen lights, like brain matter.

"I'm sorry. I saw Liore, and I just…lost it. I was mad that she didn't love me anymore."

"You never loved me and I sure as hell didn't love you," Liore said, still glued to the wall. "I loved what I thought you were."

Isobel's face reddened.

Gavin held the video screen up. Crewmen lay frozen across the screen, standing in a circle around Captain Anderson. From this vantage, they looked like dolls.

"This is what got live streamed," Gavin said.

"Should we be concerned about the authorities possibly hunting down this ship and all of us?" I asked.

"In six hours, maybe," Isobel said, "We're a long way from civilization."

Gavin tapped the screen. "Observe."

Crewmen swayed back and forth, listening to Anderson. There was no audio. The black lunchroom door swung open and "Isobel" sauntered in, immaculate except for the blood on her white gown.

Two crewmen aimed guns at "Isobel". "Isobel" held up her hands.

Something emerged from Captain Anderson's eye socket.

Colorless as a tubeworm, it thrust up and out. Blood splattered. Anderson fell to his knees. He gripped the worm-thing, pulped it, but a white tip emerged from his other eye socket, slithering out, out. He spasmed. Collapsed.

A fat crewman shot him, then dropped his gun. Growths boiled out of his ears, blooming open as they hit the air.

Flashes of gunfire. Bullets hit crewmen.

They all twitched on the floor, growths sprouting from eye sockets and mouths and various orifices. "Isobel" (Gavin, as you know) stood frozen by the door. The true Isobel entered, clad in her jumpsuit. She bent over, heaving. Gavin pulled her hair back as she dry-heaved. Watery alcohol came up.

The crewmen stopped twitching and sprouting.

Simultaneously, they stood. They climbed atop the lunchroom table. Laid down. Others piled on, forming a pyramid. Captain Anderson's cadaver scrambled to the top. He leaned back.

Then they stilled.

"Aeter," I said.

"Yes," Gavin said. "Aeter heard Anderson when he said everything was being live-streamed."

"Our skins regenerating, Liore becoming one of us, and this…display…for the humans. This entire conspiracy is more effort than I've ever seen Aeter put forth. Aeter wants the humans off Europa."

"Good," Liore said.

"Aeter could kill them all instantly if They wanted to. Why wouldn't They do that?" Gavin said.

A drawer squeaked open, then slammed. Isobel clutched a chef's knife.

"Look, I don't know what Aeter wants. I think you've got the basics right. Human society's a festering scum pit here. It was probably funny at first, but then Aeter got tired of it. Or scared they'd do what I did, capture you, steal your skin, and keep you imprisoned. This whole situation reminds me of a practice drill. Aeter wasn't showing you the skin regrowth. It was really about showing you how to escape if someone *did* steal your skin, and how easy it'd be for humans to do it," Isobel said.

"What are you doing with that knife, Isobel?" I asked.

Gavin went to comfort her, but she jerked her head from side to side. *No.*

"I don't know how this ends. Aeter's got Their millions of eyes and brains on me. Is it possible for me to die?"

"I'll find a ship or some remote outpost, and we'll take you there. You can form a new identity," Gavin said.

"Why should we do anything to help her?" Liore said.

"Good question," I said.

"I'm sorry I was too selfish to do the right thing," Isobel said.

"Oh, you're *sorry*? You're *sorry*, Isobel? That's nice. I'm sure you cried a little in your fucking mansion, in that garden you fucked me in. You find another girl the day they lobotomized me, or did you wait a week?"

Liore stared at me. "I mean, it only took you a few weeks to fuck her."

Shame flared in my chest. My skin throbbed. It wanted to *(teeth)* grow teeth, feel *(home)* water running over it, taste *(radiation)*. It was time to go Home. Dame Isobel's theatrics tired me. Liore needed education.

If Aeter truly finds you amusing, you won't be able to die, Isobel.

"I'm sorry for everything," Isobel said.

No dramatic inflections, no jaunty puns. The statement came out flat and factual. *I'm sorry. For everything.* Because she was human, she could not change. Nothing she did would ever help the victims of her family. The only thing she *could* do was exist until she aged and died. Inevitability, oblivion, death. Failure doomed every attempt she'd made to change. What else could she do? She was only what she'd been raised to be.

Dame Isobel wanted out.

I said, "Isobel—"

She lifted the knife to her throat and dragged it across.

A gash yawned open. Blood spurted. It arced and landed on the tiled floor. White ceramic tiles. Bright oxygenated blood. Knife blade greased in blood. Isobel's face remained smooth, serene. Her gaze—*so blue*—fixed on the far wall.

Gavin and Liore gaped at her.

There was nothing to do but watch Dame Isobel die, nothing I could've done to stop her, nothing I could ever do to change it.

After she died, I'd collect my old skin and slither back home with the others. Aeter would do what Aeter wanted. Isobel's family would thrive. What could I ever do to change anything? I'd been a plaything in a conspiracy the entire time.

Isobel didn't even love me.

Oh, what stupid emotions those words conjured. Love.

Spurt. Spurt. Her life reduced with each pulse.

Disgusting.

Fucking.

Alien.

Did you think that when we copulated, Isobel? Time to flee the consequences of everything. You won't be a monster. You'll die as you always wanted to, pretty and wealthy. The lost jewel of Europa. Don't worry about me or Gavin or Liore. You're dying. You can leave your worries behind, *princess.* I'm only a *disgusting fucking alien. What* do I know?

My skin tightened. Loosened. Anger spread over the skin and burned in my throat. I itched to scream.

Nothing I could do.

Why try?

In that second, I saw the inevitability of her death. There was only one true ending to this sad tale, had only ever been.

Adapt, Little One, Aeter had said, but it didn't change anything. We could bestow skin. That had changed. We could—

"What do you want, Little One?" Aeter murmured.

Want?

"If you could change anything about this, what would be different?"

I don't want her to die, I thought.

"Then do something about it."

But she's bleeding out and there's nothing I can do. I can grow skin now, but—

Oh.

Oh!

I sprinted the three steps to Isobel and clamped my hand on her throat. Blood gushed between my fingers.

I put my wrist to my teeth.

Opened.

Bit.

Teeth sharpened as I dug in, slicing through my new skin like water. I bit a portion off. Spat it into my hand. Faintly iridescent, it glimmered in the light.

I forced Isobel's mouth open and planted the skin on her tongue.

It slid for a second. Then it rooted. Threads of skin feathered off and slithered out of her lips, down to her slit-throat. Where they touched, the bleeding stopped.

Isobel stiffened in my arms.

Of course she did. I'd forced a biological version of the safety wires on her. She wanted to die pretty. And here I was, her passive little sex toy, her Fisherman, refusing her. Dame Isobel always got what she wanted.

Not anymore, Isobel.

Her lips formed syllables.

I pressed my mouth to her ear. "Oh, Isobel. You don't get to die. Not after everything you've done."

Tears flowed down her cheeks.

My skin carpeted the inside of her mouth, over her teeth, cocooning her tongue. Like a rapid-growing cancer, it multiplied. Spread. Skin clawed out of her lips and up her cheeks. It engulfed her head, wrapping that fine pearl-white hair into itself. Runners shot out from the skin, vining down her neck, curling around her arms. Spreading. Her limbs melded.

Within sixty seconds, Dame Isobel was a roughly human-sized sac of flesh, wrapped in iridescent skin.

Gavin exhaled, shuddering. Liore watched, head tilted to the side, as if all of this were a mildly entertaining fight.

I crouched down by Isobel. "I know you can hear me. I know you're in there. Go ahead, Isobel. Do it."

I extended my hand towards her.

A malformed, asymmetrical tendril formed. It strained up towards me.

She wanted something to mimic.

She didn't know how to reassemble herself into something practical. Isobel's mind remained very much intact. How horrified she must be, trapped and dissolving in new skin. She might even think I was torturing her or killing her.

I took her little sad tendril. Such a poorly made tendril. I almost told her that.

Isobel's flesh twisted into limbs and a single head. Half-melted strands of her hair melded into her cheeks and face, melted into the skin. Two eyes emerged from the morass, roughly where human eyes were supposed to be.

She'd made a copy of a copy, and she had no skill at making things at all. Only destroying. She looked like a misshapen chunk of clay with four 'limbs'. Randomly placed muscles bulged at sporadic intervals over her body.

She struggled to form a mouth.

I patted her 'face.' "We don't need to speak with words where we're going. Don't bother trying."

She shook her head. *No.*

"Yes, Isobel."

Her eyes wheeled around the room. Her lower limbs jerked. They lacked knee joints.

"This is cruel," Gavin said softly.

"She's a cruel person. Well. She isn't a person anymore, is she? She's a *disgusting fucking alien* now, like us."

Isobel's head spasmed. *NO!*

"I see you formed adequate ear canals and connected them to your brain," I said, patting her shoulder. "That's a start."

Liore Hyung giggled, the sound like an insect chittering.

"Quiet, both of you," Gavin said.

He padded to Isobel. With slow, deliberate motions, he scooped her up and carried her out. The lunchroom doors thunked.

Liore and I followed.

It would be more advantageous of me to lie to you at this point, listener. I want to say that Liore and I ventured out into the corridor with Gavin. He was crooning to Isobel, *my friend, my friend,* and it seemed to soothe her. She didn't spasm. At some point, he shared a few genetic memories with her, allowing her to shift into something that could survive home. The bilgewater doors groaned open, then shut with a ship-shaking *crack.* I imagine they went out that way.

If you like, pretend we went home alongside them.

Would you like the truth?

Liore and I stayed in the lunchroom and feasted on the human cadavers.

No ceremony, no solemnities. No half-baked eulogies for the crewmen. We left enough behind for the families to recognize them, but—as you will have seen—not much else. After everything we'd been through, we wanted to have *fun.* What a human concept. Fun is just another moniker for inefficiency.

Our feast culminated with us throwing human livers at each other, dodging and laughing when we managed to hit each other. *Splat!* Livers, blood-filled and squishy. They went *gloosh.* They painted us in red. Liore's real laugh emerged—nasally and abrasive.

As Dame Isobel would ask—is it so terrible to want a little fun?

I wouldn't mind tasting blood again.

EPILOGUE

I end the recording.

Liore smiles, wrapped in my old skin. It could be a house for her. It's that large. A home of flesh.

"Did you copy and absorb the millions of forms?" I ask.

"Yep."

"Come out, then. I need to destroy it."

She crawls out, glistening with mucous. I've copied and encoded the genetic memories for myself already. There's nothing left to save.

"Why?" Liore asks.

"The humans will run experiments on it if I don't. They don't deserve free knowledge."

I douse my old skin in lighter fluid. I step back, light a match, and toss it on. Fire surges over the skin. The stench of burning fish fills X-520.

Thump. Thump.

The ship shakes with each *thump*. My Friend's getting impatient. They've shed the Gavin form. Now they hold the ENS *Princess* between their tentacles and knock on the side.

Thump.

I shut the door behind me. It will take a long time for the fire to spread. Will the recording survive? I put the recording device in a waterproof valuables box composed of low-density plastic. According to the package, it floats.

I wander up to the viewing room, and my Friend presses themselves against the glass window. Sixty white eyes swivel to me; eyes like pearls, jewels embedded in my Friend's flesh.

Thump. Thump.

"I'm coming," I say.

Isobel must be somewhere nearby. I'll find her. Eventually. I won't apologize, but I'll tell her the truth. *You would always be a monster to them, Isobel. So I made you a freer monster. I didn't want you to die. I care about you.*

Maybe, just maybe, she'll forgive me.

We'll start with small acts of terrorism.

Liore might crawl atop the ice, form herself into a human, sabotage a water-processing plant, and slither back home.

Your society should value its members more, we might say.

Maybe I'll slither up a drain into the water supply of the Dame Family. Slither down a gullet, small as a maggot, thin as a pinworm. Destroy them from the inside out. Then out of the blood, down another drain, into the Gariellus family's water. Then the Sano Family's. They will either comply or die.

Make the lobotomies and executions stop, we'll demand.

Liore wishes she didn't remember her lobotomy. Aeter doesn't grant her wish.

My Friend might infiltrate the scientists. We don't know. We haven't worked out the details. So many *maybes.* Maybe the live-streamed footage of the lunchroom carnage won't immediately cause panic. Maybe it will.

Everything can change. Inevitability is a lie. Just when you think you know the future, that you've managed to grasp forward in time and figure it out, it mutates into something different.

Thump. Thump.

"I know," I say, "I'm being inefficient. Let me enjoy it."

I nod to Liore. Her form softens, changes. She grows, eyes bubbling, tendrils sprouting.

I knock on the window.

Thunk-thunk.

Our signal.

My Friend tears the ENS *Princess* apart.

SCREEEECH!

I slip into my summer form—

Cracks spiderweb the viewing room window. The seam where metal meets window splits. Europa's atmosphere claws in, bringing cold. Air streams out.

Instead of killing me, the cold soothes.

Broken glass slicing into my tentacles, I haul myself outside. Teetering on the edge of the ship, I pause.

Isobel.

I have to see what I've done.

I let go and fall.

Impact.

A splash. Chunks of ice fly.

Then I'm Home.

Isobel, I call, and an answering song wavers through the water.

I don't know what will happen next.

Home cradles me. Salt and water and ice, the endless swirling dance of flesh, of change and life. For this moment, I exist without pain. I believe Isobel does, too.

Instead of waiting to find out, I move towards the song.

Isobel?

Isobel.

THE END

ACKNOWLEDGMENTS

Thank you to everyone that helped me with this quirky sapphic sci-fi novella!

Thank you to Ai Jiang and Bonnie Jo Stufflebeam for reading this novella and blurbing it. Your kind words meant so much to me. Special thanks to Evangeline Gallagher for illustrating the awesome cover.

To Candace Nola: Thank you for encouraging me throughout the editing process, and so many other times.

To Brennan LaFaro: Thanks for reading this weird lil novella, man. Appreciate it.

To Briana Morgan: Thank you for reading this and supporting me throughout everything.

Special thanks to my ARC readers. You guys are awesome! Thank you to everyone else who helped make *Landlocked in Foreign Skin* a reality.

Chapter One

"ALL I WANTED WERE those bodies, Jennifer-baby," the Divine Flesh said. "Just those silly little cadavers. Or even just *one* cadaver. Why do you keep hurting Me?"

I woke up in a ditch, which wasn't so bad. The Divine Flesh didn't stop talking. She never stops talking.

"Jennifer-baby, I want to create," She said.

The ditch rutted either side of some county road. Cracks marred asphalt, webbing the road's lines. Tumbleweeds filled the ditch, forming a river of dead and desiccated plants. All the midsummer grasses were here: cheatgrass, sagebrush, goatheads. Bits of cheatgrass itched inside my jeans. Farther back from the road, cherry orchards rowed the land, green enough to burn my eyes. It smelled green, like weeds and grass and dirt . White-hot noon blazed over cherry orchards and washed out the gold hills on the horizon.

Ash coated my hands—

—he's in the beige bathtub when She finds him, all alone in his mobile home except for the yipping worried Chihuahua, he's lying in the red red water, so very pale, the slit on his thigh hanging open, exposing treasures, the white sliver of his femur; he tastes like sweat and ethyl alcohol and tears. She bundles his flesh to Herself, She's crying, She repairs the wound and he lives again, She licks the suicide-blood off him and bathes him instead in love, asks him gently, Would you be Mine? But it's a silly question, the answer's always yes, yes, and so She sanctifies his flesh as his little dog chatters—

—The Divine Flesh had taken control of our shared body and revived some random dude. Great. Fantastic. I staggered to my feet. I picked under a nail.

The Divine Flesh cooed, "And then he was SO happy!"

"He's dead."

"He *was* dead, silly. Until I recreated him. God, you're depressed. I didn't hurt anyone."

I sucked gore out from under my nails. Salty-sweet. Blood.

"Be quiet and think. What time is it? We're supposed to be at Daryl's tonight," I said.

Even saying that made my heart beat faster.

"I'll tell you if you let Me out."

"You had your fun last night."

"Fine, then. I'll tell you if you let Me *show you* some of what I made. Take a look," She said.

I did not take a look. I did not ask to be shown whatever fresh horror She'd molded out of a casualty list, and for once, the Divine Flesh didn't play show and tell. I dug into my pockets. C'mon, God. I need cash. Jesus loves me, this I know, so can I find a twenty or even a C-note, here? A gift card to Denny's?

My pockets were empty.

Current inventory: one dirty Metallica tank top. One pair of stained—*bloodstained, Jennifer, let's not kid ourselves*—skinny jeans. No socks. No shoes. No purse, phone, wallet, or money, but also no corpses...within sight. The road gaped. I stuck my thumb out for luck.

Let me make you something, She thought.

Suddenly, the smell of bacon. Heat shot through my jaw. A rush of saliva filled my mouth. That wasn't good. It meant She currently had enough power to control my senses. She could make me see things, hear things, smell things...and if She felt like it, make me see a stable patch of ground instead of a cliff, a green traffic signal instead of a red, or whatever creative way She could think of to kill me. Then She'd take control of our body. Again.

I had to distract the Divine Flesh.

"You wanna help? Tell me where we are, and how we got here," I said.

"Don't remember. You've got the part that thinks about all those silly things like spatial distance and time. When you're not burying our brain in...chemicals?" She fished for the word. "...drugs."

"It's Thursday. We're supposed to be at Daryl's at six."

Yes, think about Daryl. You love Daryl. We're going to see Daryl.

"Let Me out. I can get us anywhere in five minutes, babygirl. I see where the skin's thin," the Divine Flesh said.

"Absolutely not."

She giggled. "Have it your way. You're the one who's in trouble with Daryl, not Me. He loves Me."

I waited by the side of the road for a few minutes before a fruit truck, laden with splintered crates of Rainier cherries, slowed. The wrinkled driver smiled at me. An easy, howdy-missy smile.

"Need a ride, ma'am?"

I smiled back, hands on hips. "Appreciate it, thanks."

So far, so good. If Mr. American Farmer wanted sex as payment, I'd have expected nothing less. I would have done a good job of it. I don't put my thumb out if I'm not prepared to suck someone off for the car ride. Believe me—I've done worse.

"Hop in," he said. "Name's Clay."

I used my standard fake name. "I'm Molly."

I entered. It smelled like dust and soured fermented fruit.

Don't worry, The Divine Flesh thought. *If he tries to hurt you, I'll protect you.*

I'm not worried for me. I'm worried for him, I thought.

She laughed. *You're so silly.*

The fruit truck jolted over a bump.

"You okay?" Clay asked, cigarette between his lips.

No, random American farmer, I wasn't.

Sometimes it would almost burst out of me, in moments like these. Freakazoid Jennifer, freakazoid me, so self-destructive that any semi-kind statement made her chest ache. Sometimes I liked to pretend someone was listening. I'd snap, make some sappy, tear-ridden emotional monologue about my life and my problems, and they'd listen. They'd care.

They'd ask, *Jennifer, what's wrong?*

I've got a flesh-bending cosmic goddess trapped in my skin, and both of us hate each other.

Holy shit! Jennifer, how long's that been going on?

In my earliest memory, I'm three years old, sitting on cold, kitchen linoleum. Sitting in a pool of blood. Two dead bodies lie on the water-stained floor nearby. Bio Mom and Dad. It smells like speed. Speed's crackling in an old used two-liter bottle in the trailer sink, because they're using the Shake 'N Bake of cookin' speed, no lab needed. Chemicals fizz in the bottle. It's bulging from gas buildup. Nobody's loosening the cap every five minutes to let the gases out. Soon, it'll explode, splattering the trailer and three-year-old me with caustic, dangerous liquid— basically Drano. Products line the kitchen counter: Sudafed, instant cold packs, camp-stove propane, fertilizer, Drano... other stuff, too. Spice bottles roll across the floor: McCormick

Salad Magic and Poultry Seasoning, desiccated bay leaves in their jar, the pretty spices I want to touch and smell because the chemicals stink. My nose burns. My cheeks burn, raw from crying. And the Divine Flesh is there, shushing me like an older sister. She soothes, *They wanted to hurt you. It's okay, babygirl. I'll always, always be here. FOREVER. I LOVE YOU!*

My listener would ask, *Jennifer, have you tried therapy? Antidepressants? Prescribed drugs instead of self-medicating?*

Jennifer, are you insane?

I'd laugh. I'd tell them about all the times I've died. I'd tell them that a shotgun blast to the head hurts less than a bullet. I'd march them over to Daryl Plummer's storage unit in Coeur d'Alene, pull out the black plastic storage bin marked *Jennifer's Body*, and show them the wet-preserved fragments that the Divine Flesh bequeathed to him when he was in that creepy taxidermy phase. I'd dust off the jars and juxtapose them against my body.

The Divine Flesh crawls in my skin, but She's kind enough to repair the damage.

Jennifer, you wouldn't, like, kill yourself or anything, right? You're not gonna pull a Jesus-Savior thing?

Jennifer, you're self-destructive.

This is where we'd start fighting, and then it'd get too heated.

The Divine Flesh would possess me, rip out their throat or heart, and transmute them into, like, an eldritch horse or something. No matter how much I begged Her not to.

"You look like you just took a shit and saw your liver floatin' in the toilet," Clay said.

"If someone gave you one last chance to redeem yourself, and you might've blown it because you got drunk and then woke up on the side of a road in the middle of nowhere, how would you feel?"

"You need some of those AA meetings?"

"Where am I? What time is it?"

He jerked his thumb at the dashboard. Duct tape held a cheap wristwatch to the left of the radio. The clock hands said 12:30.

"Can I have a smoke?" I asked.

"Ain't good for your body."

"Do I look healthy?"

His muddy eyes scanned along my arms. Dash-shaped scars meshed every inch of their skin, rowing from armpits to wrists, each one about a quarter-inch long. The colors ranged from silvery to cherry-red.

"Can I have a smoke, pretty please? I'm legal," I said.

"Center compartment."

I fished around a pile of dusty receipts and glass vials. A molar rotted in a corner of the compartment, dotted in dried blood. Cigs spilled out of a crushed Marlboro pack. I selected one, rescued a BIC lighter, and lit it. Drew in smoke.

"Lotta orchards. We in Washington?" I asked.

"Yakima. You got a home?"

I kept expecting him to reach over. Waited for the hand on my thigh.

"Y'know, I gotta say, I ain't all that impressed with you," he said, rubbing his age-spotted jaw. "It's cherry season."

I blinked.

Cherry season.

Something tickled the back of my brain. Why...did last night seem so important? I mean, beyond the need to get high —that was a given. Teeth. Teeth in glass vials. Exonumia, slicked in blood. Dixie cups half-filled with pinkish slime, spit, water. Pliers on a table, pliers grasped in non-hand appendages. A forked tongue, working between my thighs. Pleasure. Rough, slick texture. A rowdy butch's voice, telling me about Spine and good hard whiskey. If we went to another place, there'd be better stuff. She wasn't a Mirror Person; I let her fuck me. Her forked tongue worked and worked, *so good, keep going,* and her hair was banana-candy yellow, cropped close to her skull.

I probed an empty space in my gums that hadn't been there yesterday.

Another fragment of last night flickered by. *Cherries.* Maraschino cherries, bobbing in last night's pineapple upside-down cake cocktail like bloated corpses. I'd been talking about a job, a shipment of something. Cute forked-tongue butch said, *Listen for cherries, Jennifer. You're holding the shipment for a few days, then taking them to—*

"These cherries are goin' to Mesa, Arizona," Clay said, and his grip tightened on the steering wheel.

So this was why I'd ended up here. I'd gotten blitzed, gotten bored, taken a job, trekked off into the night, accidentally let the Divine Flesh loose, and then collapsed at the pickup rendezvous.

"Kinda funny," I said.

"Hm?"

"If this is a shipping route for the orchards, where are the other fruit trucks? Road should be full of 'em, Clay."

"You figure it out, *Jennifer*?"

I nodded. "Want me to drop you off in a better location before I take over—"

"No."

He swallowed. Hard. The flesh on his neck jiggled.

"Doesn't have to be your house. Or anywhere associated with you, your family, or your friends. It can be the next gas station we drive past," I said.

"You don't gotta."

I exhaled smoke. "I don't like leaving people in the middle of nowhere. It's bad for morale. Shitty business practice."

"You care?"

"More than I should," I said.

"You're the Flesh Failure. I don't want you caring 'bout me, understand?" he said.

Cornfields rippled on both sides of the freeway, crowned with green silk. I cranked the window down. July air, humid. Thick with the gamey smell of growing things and pesticide. Rainier cherry season. Too early for Bings.

"I won't even remember your face or name, trust me," I said.

None of it mattered. Mr. American Farmer's name wasn't actually Clay. He wasn't human, and I wasn't moving a shipment of cherries.

Most likely, I'd be safeguarding a clutch of parasitic babies from vigilante exterminators. Or bits of dried Mirror Person, called, uncreatively, Spine. Or plain vanilla fentanyl. You move a lot of fentanyl in rural areas.

I never said I was a good person.

I crushed out my cig. "Spine or babies?"

"Both," he said. "Eggs. Not larvae."

Jennifer, I wanna DO THINGS, the Divine Flesh whined.

I thought, *Okay, what brand of non-human is this guy?*

She thought, *He tastes like one of the Mirror People. He has skin cells. He's shedding them off and I can TASTE the dust. I like it. I wanna clothe him in something slippery. He'd look better—*

Mirror People.

My guts clenched.

You should feel sorry for 'em. But I don't. Mirror People are genderless, supercoiled silvery wasp-like beings with the "empathy" of a billion saccharine therapists hopped up on pure oxytocin. They reflect the environment around them, changing their appearance and bodies at will. Mirror People are great. Super nice. Until they go into heat, lose their hyper-empathy, and go into sociopath mode, looking for some poor victim to impregnate with their larvae. They don't like to talk about where they're from. The most I ever got out of one was: *God decided to end reality. We had to leave. Now we're here.*

I ignored the Divine Flesh, as usual. I checked a mental padlock, tugged at it. Saw Her contained and docile. For now. She kept trying to get my attention. She kept saying that Clay didn't taste quite right, but I tuned Her out.

Crates rattled as the truck jostled over pitted road.

"Where is it?" I asked.

"Glovebox."

I opened it. Two prescription pill bottles lurked inside. Flyspecks of dried blood covered the labels. A potpourri bag of something called *Lavender Summer* rested under the insurance papers. Not a clever repack, but standard for Mirror People. Spine looks almost identical to dried lavender. Think potpourri at Grandma's crack house.

I lifted a pill bottle.

Mirror-Person eggs shone near to the brim. They gleamed like pellets of chrome, small as aspirin.

"How many in each bottle?" I asked.

"Sixty. A hundred-twenty total."

He pulled off the road, let the truck idle. We switched drivers.

The fruit stand came up as we continued. *Cherries! Rainiers! Antiques!* proclaimed painted plywood signs.

I drove into the fruit stand's parking area

"Crates are for show. You can hock 'em or burn 'em or what have you."

"All right."

Five hour drive from here to Daryl's.

Something fluttered in my chest.

I could still meet up with Daryl. I could still save this. As long as I drove continuously and nothing went wrong. It'd been a whole year since we'd talked. Since he'd kicked me out. Would he look different? Would his new friends think I was okay? What did Daryl say when he talked about me?

Jennifer, yeah, my ex, she's a junkie.

Jennifer's a mess.

Oh, we knew each other back from the foster care system. Way back. She's been the same self-destructive, scar-covered piece of shit that she was when I met her at fourteen.

I needed a different life motto. "No drug left undone" was really starting to fry my brain.

Clay opened the truck door. Then he hesitated, dug in his shirt pocket, and thrust a twenty at me. It smelled like cinnamon Altoids.

"Here. Git somethin' to eat," he said.

"Aw, shit. You don't have to—"

"The hell I don't. You're skin and bones."

Is he implying that I STARVE YOU? the Divine Flesh snapped. *Because it's not My fault I forget to feed our body when I go create My children.*

"Thanks," I said.

Clay grunted approval. Then he practically sprinted out of the truck, gnawing his lip. The Divine Flesh tapped on the door of Her mental prison, saying, *You didn't even see the things I created in Tieton, babygirl.*

Clay became engulfed in the standard fruit-stand crowd: tourists clad in bland designer clothing and cooing over half-rotten past-season strawberries, sour-faced grandmothers yanking grandkids over to the pickling cukes, and fecund young fundamentalist families with smartphones and their broods, wearing nervous expressions—*Is this where you go to get produce for Instagram posts on slow living?* Around piles of rusted iron antiques, men long past their prime smoked Camels and wheezed, cancer gestating in their lungs.

I drove on. Why watch "Clay" homogenize?

***

Can you redeem the sins of the flesh?

I cranked up the religious radio stations, for variety. I had a five-hour drive. I spent a lot of it thinking and drinking peach-flavored Monsters.

You had that fight.

You were high! It was over a year ago! Anyway, it was all Her fault.

If someone lived in a trailer in the forest by their ex's cabin, because he kicked them out a year ago, because apparently throwing plates was "inexcusable" now, but it was partly driven by the emotions of the meat-bending horror inside their body… would they still be redeemable?

Cloudless sky loomed over me. Sweat slimed my thighs.

Daryl must've thought so.

It'd been a quick phone call from him, a week ago. He'd said, "Hey. Emily and Javier are coming over on Thursday. You wanna meet them?"

Then me, taking a solid thirty seconds to respond. "What?"

"Not as lovers…Jennifer, I miss you."

Neither of us brought up the Divine Flesh. It was better that way.

I said, "Yeah, me too. It's just—Hey, you get custody of the kids?"

"I'm not going to be involved in your lifestyle anymore," he said, in that blunt Daryl-way of his. "No more drugs, none of that. I miss you. Emily and Javier want to meet you, bring you into the fold, you know how it is out here in the boonies."

"My *lifestyle?* Oh my god, Daryl. You bought my supplies and Sudafed when I needed to cook a batch of speed and I was too fucked up to go out in public. You're not the Jesse to my Walter White, asshole. You handed ten high-schoolers thirty bucks to buy a pack of Sudafed for you and told them to keep the change, and then you went to Lowe's for the fertilizer and plastic tubing. For fuck's sake—"

Daryl's voice chilled. "That was enough to keep me from getting custody of Marcia and Isaac when the cops came."

"Hey, I'm sorry. So sorry. So, so very sorry. I'm just Evil Fucking Jennifer, right? I magically possessed you like a demon and made you cook speed with me all these years. Me. I guess I'm fucking magical now--"

"Forget I called," he said.

"—because you had *no control* of your body, right, Daryl?"

My face had burned, and my heart kept pounding in my ears. I tasted metal.

"You had—" and my voice broke. "No control. Right? Just couldn't control yourself."

"I'm sorry you're dealing with the Divine Flesh."

"What the fuck did you think was gonna happen when you called me, Daryl? I'd tell you I still love you?"

He sighed. "I shouldn't have cheated on you."

"You finally called it what it is. Cheating."

"Can we—look, Jennifer. You're my oldest buddy. I wouldn't be alive if it wasn't for you. You know I don't got family I talk to anymore. You're it. The closest thing I got to family."

"Same," I whispered.

"Do you wanna come over and meet Emily and Javier?"

"Okay. Okay."

"Can you try to be sober?"

"Yeah," I said, because sober meant hope. I could do that.

I missed Daryl. So much. So I drove, and I thought about that little snippet of hope I had left. There was a chance. All I had to do was get to Daryl's cabin at six. I had time. I had hope.

I really did.

Until I hit Moscow, Idaho, and the fruit truck's rear tire blew out at 5:01 p.m., exactly an hour and a half away from Daryl's cabin.

Shit.

WANT TO SEE WHAT HAPPENS NEXT?

Preorder THE DIVINE FLESH!

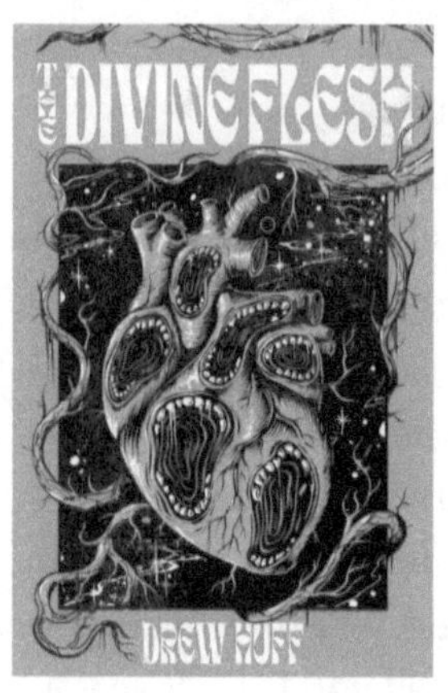

ABOUT THE AUTHOR

Drew Huff is the author of *Free Burn*, *Landlocked in Foreign Skin*, and *The Divine Flesh*. Born and raised in eastern Washington, she writes fantastical horror and speculative tales about trauma, humanity, and body horror. Her short fiction has appeared in numerous anthologies, including *The Sacrament, It Was All A Dream*, and *Hot Iron and Cold Blood*. For more information, visit her website at drewehuff.com

Instagram: @druhuf
X: @dreadnought_dru

X ⓞ

THANK YOU FOR READING! LIKE THIS BOOK?

You can make my day great by leaving a review on Amazon, Goodreads, or any social media!

As a bonus, it also helps other potential readers find this story.

Thanks again for reading!

www.ingramcontent.com/pod-product-compliance
Lightning Source LLC
Chambersburg PA
CBHW061542310726
48972CB00008B/2578